Breathe

Between the Lines

Dalene Reyburn

www.dalenereyburn.com

ISBN 978-0-620-88082-4 eBook ISBN 978-0-620-88081-7

Printed in South Africa

All Scripture quotations, unless otherwise indicated, are taken from the *Holy Bible, New Living Translation* ® Copyright © 1996, 2004, 2007 by Tyndale House Foundation. Used by permission of Tyndale House Publishers, Inc., Carol Stream, Illinois 60188. All rights reserved.

Editing and wild cheering: Murray Reyburn, Shirley Noel, Carin Mascini
Typesetting: Tanja Dunstan
Cover design: Duncan Reyburn and Heather Jenkins
Author photo: Cameron Reyburn
Marketing and promotion: Kurt Schröder of *Double Shift*
Audiobook recording: Damian Phillips

For Lené, who taught me how to

b r e a t h e.

'Every Scripture has been written by the Holy Spirit, the breath of God. It will empower you by its instruction and correction, giving you the strength to take the right direction and lead you deeper into the path of godliness.'

2 Timothy 3:16, TPT

Contents

Note to reader

This is a work of fiction. Certain longstanding institutions, agencies, public figures and historical events are mentioned, but the characters involved are wholly imaginary. Any resemblance to persons living or dead is coincidental. The opinions expressed are those of the characters and should not be confused with the author's. The characters you will meet on these pages, you will never meet in real life. However, it is the author's hope that you will meet – in real life – the very real God who is sovereign over every story, including yours.

November
2 0 1 4

'Everybody is a book of blood; wherever we're opened, we're red.'

Clive Barker

1

Cape Town

*'There's nothing like a printed book;
the weight, the woody scent, the feel, the look.'*

E.A. Bucchianeri

No one else calls me Kit Kat.

That's what went through her mind the same time the bullet went through her body.

Kayla Ray was a regular at Trend – a café every bit what its name suggested. It had appropriately chic sensory combinations of unvarnished wood and gleaming chrome and indie folk rock and indigenous succulents. Hipster baristas scrawled people's names on recycled cardboard cups rough enough to convince earth-conscious patrons they were *literally* improving the planet one cappuccino at a time.

She usually drank Americanos. Today she ordered a Sprite to celebrate summer. The streets had been sticky with slow irritated traffic, but it was totally worth the petrol it cost to drive from the university to Camps Bay. Totally worth the stop-start frustration of finding a parking spot. From a shady table out front she could almost ignore Victoria Road – sweating with tourists – and breathe in the sea.

She reached into her bag for a Bible. Flipped it open. It wore a brown, faux leather cover, fitted slenderly over the book itself. She slipped two fingers deep inside the front cover and pulled out the card hidden there – dog-eared with love and re-reading.

2006-11-26

My Kit Kat

Happy birthday.

This comes with so much love to you, as you keep on keeping on, along God's way. What lies ahead for you is anyone's guess, but your Heavenly Father has plotted your course, and He promises this in Psalm 48:14: 'He is our God forever and ever, and He will guide us until we die.'

Life has its ups and downs, and you'll probably experience suffering, shame and rejection. You'll likely be tempted towards rebellion, anger or fear. It's then, in your quest to be free of those things, that you'll need to dig deep for God's truth, so you can discover possibility, purpose, grace, healing, transformation, peace, hope and love – and ultimately, God's glory, and the advancement of His Kingdom, because that's the point of it all.

Keep doing the next right thing – even if that just means taking the next deep breath. Travel light. Don't be afraid to walk off the map. The view is always better from the road less travelled – and life is either a daring adventure, or nothing at all. May His joy be your strength, every step.

Love always,

Grampa

PS: Here's a list of my 'life verses'. Perhaps you'll enjoy looking them all up, and making them your own.

Kayla loved the arts, though she wasn't artistic. Optimistically auditioning for countless plays and musicals at school and varsity, she'd always bagged minor one-liner roles because even by a generous stretch of the kindest imagination, she was no actress. But if she ever needed to pull off a weepy part, she could just pull out her grampa's card before walking on stage. It never failed to make her tear-up.

She did the emotional Math of the past decade, her mind's eye scanning years like abacus beads. The Bible had been a gift for her sixteenth birthday. She'd be twenty-four in a week and her grandfather had been gone just over a year.

She'd loved that holiday. Just her, gran and grampa. They'd done it for each grandkid's sixteenth birthday. A long weekend trip to the Kruger National Park. Gran turned steaks on the braai – she was better at it than anyone – while she and grampa sat on a bench overlooking the Letaba River. He handed over the Bible: unwrapped, covered in love. Then blew his nose and announced more loudly than was necessary that he should probably help gran with the steaks though they both knew that was ridiculous.

She tucked the card – deep and snug for safekeeping – into the Bible's front cover once again as her phone pinged her back to the present and her table at Trend. Mom.

Hello sweetie, class go ok?

Kayla was a tutor in the English Department of the University of Cape Town. Occasionally she filled in for professors who were off delivering papers at conferences during which they felt inclined to adopt a British accent. Today had been a tough ask. A discussion of the theme of the complexity of human relationships in Virginia Woolf's *To the Lighthouse*, with a class of second-years – equal parts bra-burning feminists and angsty academics.

She was about to reply when her Sprite arrived.

'Thanks Goodwin.'

She knew most of the Trend staff – made a point of glancing at their badges and using their names. Her mother had been fierce about that when Kayla and her brothers were growing up. *Look people in the eye! Greet and ask and thank by name!* She remembered being annoyed, as a teenager, to see how right her mother had been. How windows of the world opened to you when you bothered to really see people.

Trend didn't offer straws – plastic or paper. They were saving the oceans *and* the trees. She brought the glass to her lips and thought about her own name. Kayla was a white, skinny name. Translucent like Sprite. It was a name that went to a Joburg private school and had highlights and a manicure with the ring finger painted glittery. It was draped thinly over her, she felt. She imagined how it might feel to have a dark, robust name she could sink her teeth into. A name she could wear with bright colours, romance and intrigue.

That's why she loved that grampa had picked something chocolatey. *Kit Kat.*

'Enjoy,' Goodwin smiled.

Goodwin had served them here a couple weeks ago when she'd convinced Jordan they needed the sea breeze to cool off, in every way.

'He's so beautifully Zimbabwean,' she'd said, glancing at Goodwin as he swerved deftly between tables, laden tray held aloft.

'What?'

'I'm just saying he's obviously Zimbabwean. Not just his name. He's got those unmistakeable Shona features. Warm. Open.'

'Kayla, Kayla, Kayla,' said Jordan like she was a cute but recalcitrant toddler. 'Really? You're stooping to racial profiling?'

This was fast becoming a relationship trait: Jordan seizing her innocent observations as opportunities to criticize and condescend.

'Racial pro – *what?* Jords, it's not racial profiling to notice where another human comes from. If I said, *I bet Goodwin doesn't have a work permit*, that would be racial profiling. But I didn't *say* that and he *does* have one because he wasn't here last week and Adrian told me he was at Home Affairs – '

'Ok-ok, chill.'

He'd watched her with something of a smirk. As if he enjoyed seeing her take the bait.

The back of her neck stiffened hot and cross. *Chill. Just chill,* she told herself now, sipping her Sprite and flicking over abacus beads in her mind again. It had been over between her and Jordan for a week. And she was so glad. Sad. Hurt. Annoyed. Slightly bewildered. But mostly glad.

The tension hadn't been all politics and philosophy.

She'd fallen hard for his easy-going charm. They'd met at a twenty-first neither of them particularly wanted to be at, flirting and bonding over the weird décor and mediocre food. He'd unleashed in her an insouciance she'd never really known. He made her feel beautiful and, for the first time ever, cool enough.

Initially – smitten and eager to please her – he'd played the game. He came with her to church. He visited her life group when he didn't have club hockey or tutoring as an excuse, and her friends sparkled under his attention almost as much as she did.

But as weeks turned into months and their relationship found its rhythm, he'd found more and more reasons to go drinking with mates come Friday night, and fewer and fewer reasons to hang out with her.

When he did come over to her flat, things would steam up uncontrollably. He wanted sex. She didn't.

Well. She wanted sex. In fact, she very much looked forward to it. Just not now. Not yet. Not like this. And the more he teased and mocked and manipulated and coerced, the more defensive and sardonic she got.

'I'm not a prude, babe. Just a virgin. Sorry for actually, like, having convictions, and like, actually believing in like, actual marriage!'

Then he'd leave and she'd emotionally kick herself for letting it all bring out the bitch in her. (And worse – the petulant, sarcastic bitch.) For letting him undermine her dreams of doing it right.

But the truth nagged at her gut until it was too loud to ignore. She was settling. She had to end it.

So after a horrible conversation in the visitors' parking area of her apartment block close to UCT, involving a lot of tears (both of them) and some shouting (mostly Kayla) and blaming (mostly Jordan) then more tears (Jordan) and muted apologies (Kayla) and ardent professions of love (Jordan) and an overturned pot plant (Jordan) and final friend-zoning (Kayla) – it was over.

She took another Sprite sip and tapped a quick reply to her mom –

Survived! Just recovering at Trend ☺ Chat tonight xxx

Then she sighed out the breath-prayer that was becoming a fixture in her thoughts –

Comfort me.

She'd been reading bits of Isaiah. Even understanding some of it. She flipped to the end of the book – then back a page – chapter sixty-five – scanned the text – distracted. Her brothers used to tease her for being such a highlighter nerd and her Bible was serious evidence. She'd trawled through the dozens of verses her grampa had listed for her, making life-verse discoveries of her own along the way, and from Genesis to Revelation there were passages dyed bright. Scribblings and underlinings. Dates and notes and question marks.

The verse caught her. Verse twenty-four. She read and re-read. Highlighted. Read it again.

Wow wow wow.

She'd prayed for comfort. He hadn't taken long.

The smile still played at her lips when she heard chairs fall – a table skid

– screams.

Out here on the café deck, she'd been facing the sea – her back turned away from where the men must have come right past her – off the street – across the terrace – into the café.

The commotion wrenched her from the prophet on the pages. She spun round. Four men – balaclavas – guns. They were shouting –

'Get down!'

'Don't move!'

Then shouting to each other in something Kayla didn't understand. Her Xhosa was passable. She had a bit of Zulu. They weren't speaking either.

Instinctively she fell to the ground – crouched beneath the table – arms over her head.

That's when her world went slow-motion quiet. Cowering low she glanced across the café. Two women lay on the floor a metre from her. One was sobbing. Gasping. *Asthma attack?* She held a baby. *A baby!* One of the waiters – *Goodwin?* – his back turned to her – lay up against them like a human sandbag. She saw a glass smash to the floor but she couldn't hear it. At another table someone's MacBook was still playing what looked like an Ed Sheeran clip. Earphones dangled abandoned.

One of the gunmen must've gone into the kitchen. The staff were being shuffled out, shaking visibly. Arms hunched over their faces. Shoved to the floor.

The men were dangerously afraid – yelling at the customers – yelling at each other. The one closest to her turned to the street, unhinged terror in his eyes.

It's happening, came the incredulous thought to Kayla's brain. *This is happening.*

Then –

Why's no one coming? Why's no one COMING?

17

Then –

Phone. Phone someone. Phone.

Barely unfolding herself from her trembling position she leaned onto the seat of her chair. Her phone was on the table next to her Sprite. If she could just reach up – quick – and grab –

Suddenly the shouting was street side –

'*Hey wena! Hayi! Biza amapolisa!*'

Kayla turned to see the car guard she'd tipped to keep an eye on her Suzuki. He was freaking out – calling for the police – calling for the gunmen to stop –making his way through parked cars on the pavement – voice wild with fear – '*Hayi! Stop!*'

Kayla panicked. No one was coming – and now someone was coming – but she'd seen the look in that gunman's eyes.

No, she thought. *No no no! Keep away!* And the face of her grandfather and his soft chuckle and how he was the only one who called her Kit Kat.

Then a simultaneous crack and more screams and pain ripping right through the middle of everything.

***

Mom.

It was the first thing that drifted through the dark and gathered vague coherence. Her mom's voice. And –

Why's mom crying?

'But – how bad? I mean will she ever be able to – will she – '

The voice broke off. Muffled sobs. Then not so muffled.

Oh boy. Ugly cry. Where –

Then a voice she didn't know.

'She's coming round.'

'Sweetie?'

'Kayla, I'm Dr Dreyer.' A woman's voice. Young. 'You're at Mediclinic. Can you hear me, Kayla?'

Kayla's thoughts swirled unconvinced. She tried again to open her eyes. So dry. Her mouth was so dry.

'Kayla can you tell me the last thing you remember?'

Remember. What?

She was cold. There was a horrible throbbing somewhere in her head. In her stomach. She couldn't feel her fingers. Or could she? So confused.

But mom's in Joburg.

What happened?

Trend. Sprite. Goodwin.

Her voice was an odd rasp when she finally managed to shove language to the surface. Like she'd been licking an ashtray, her dad would've said.

'Twenty-four.'

She heard her mom's hurried tearful assurance – 'She's almost twenty-four.' Then – 'That's right my sweet; it's your birthday next week.' Her mom was stroking her arm. 'Do you remember anything from the – were you – '

'No – twenty-four. Verse. Verse twenty-four. Chapter sixty-five. Isaiah.'

She was slipping again. She felt the darkness suck her down – but not before she saw the words clearly – the words she'd read –

'I will answer them before they even call to Me. While they are still talking about their needs, I will go ahead and answer their prayers!'

2

Johannesburg

'The world was my oyster but I used the wrong fork.'

Oscar Wilde

'I'm glad you didn't have to go to Camps Bay for that coffee, beautiful.'

Thandeka Menziwa felt Craig's uniform against her bare arm. He always appeared out of nowhere, startling her with his intense attention. They were scheduled for the same flight tonight – Rio de Janeiro – taking off from O.R. Tambo's 03L/21R runway in a couple of hours.

'Huh?' she said, frowning at her paper cup. *Tandeka* in black koki – just below the Trend logo. Instead of *Thandeka*. She was used to it. White barista.

'Just heard it on 702. Apparently there was an armed robbery at the Trend in Camps Bay today. A girl was shot. A *woman*, sorry. Shot in the stomach. Stable but critical. So flippin' hectic.'

Despite his mock deference for gender sensitivity, Craig seemed genuinely concerned. He collected his order and together their shoes clip-clopped briskly through automatic doors and onto the tarmac, the way shoes of slick airline staff always do.

Thandeka slowed down slightly next to Craig. Sipped her coffee studiously. Tried to keep in step with the pilot because if she got ahead of him he would just be looking at her butt which she knew looked good in her flight attendant skirt and she was tired of secretly *wanting* him to think she looked good in her skirt and not so secretly hating herself for enjoying the actual slutty-ness of that fact.

Eish, it is what it is, she thought with a flush of shame.

She had a love-hate relationship with all the pilots who wanted to sleep with her. And she had a love-hate relationship with skirts. It was hard to admit she'd been shallow enough to use skirts – and the long legs they revealed – to get the shifts she wanted, or to work business class instead of economy (until she realised guys in business class could be even sleazier than guys in economy).

Her *gogo's* voice was stitched tight into the hems and zips of every too-short piece and there was no drowning it out. *Wena, is this who you are, Thandeka?*

But at age twenty-seven and a bit, she knew it was those very same fibres of femininity that had not only kept her life from unravelling completely over the past decade, but had sewn together her success.

Thandeka had grown up in Nkwazela, KwaZulu-Natal. Her parents died within a year of one other, before she turned three. Their death certificates gave tuberculosis as cause of death, but she knew that in Nkwazela, people didn't die of TB. Not really. People died of TB because those people had AIDS. She knew this was why *gogo* sometimes called her *simangaliso* – miracle. Because she should have died too. Anti-retroviral drugs for HIV only reached South African hospitals in 2004 – seven years after Thandeka was born by emergency C-section in the district hospital – a fact that probably prevented transmission of the virus, and saved her life.

She had the faintest recollection of her mom. A touch. The soft scent of Lux soap. She supposed her dad couldn't be unpicked from wherever he'd been tacked onto her DNA, but nothing of him remained in the threads of memory. So she was raised by her maternal grandmother, in a household of aunts and cousins and no men. The men arrived only on rare occasions, carrying mysteriously powerful auras of faraway Gauteng jobs, and wanting food and beer. And skirts.

Her *gogo* was devout and disciplined, and she expected no less from those who, willingly or not, fell under her iron rule. She exacted flawless obedience to curfews and dress codes from Thandeka and her cousins. Yet it was no secret how fiercely relentless her love was, and how deep her belief that her grandchildren's future needn't be defined by their past. She worked ten-hour days – straddled by two-hour commutes – to make sure Thandeka could board at Pietermaritzburg Girls' High School where she got a good Matric.

It wasn't good enough for a scholarship and there was no money for university, so Thandeka applied for corporate funding to go to flight attendant school, and the interview gave her the first taste of her feminine forces. She was pretty sure she got the job because she looked hot in her skirt. Her cousin, Nofoto, had bussed with her all the way to Joburg – for moral support, but mostly to see the city. She had dragged Thandeka into the ladies' bathroom five minutes before the interview, and safety-pinned her hem a little higher like a pro.

'No one's gonna know!' Nofoto had giggled. It was just shorter than *gogo* would like. Just long enough not to be trashy. Just perfect to get attention.

Thandeka knew *gogo* still prayed for her every single day. Guilt twisted her gut. Lately she was tired of the tight rope. Trying to please the airline and get ahead. Trying to please God and get to heaven. God didn't speak to her much, but when He did, He sounded a lot like *gogo*.

She and Craig boarded the aircraft and she tossed her empty coffee cup in the galley and wondered briefly about the girl who'd been shot and if she'd ordered the same flat white as Thandeka and if Cape Town baristas spelled people's names right and if the shot girl also wore skirts to get ahead.

Then she busied herself down an aisle – ignoring the banter of the other flight attendants – leaning in towards every other seat pouch to straighten the inflight magazine. *Find your freedom,* shouted the cover, words splashed across an impossible sunset and endless lavender fields in the south of France.

Ha. Wouldn't that be great. France.

She sighed.

And freedom.

3

Cape Town

'These mountains that you are carrying, you were only supposed to climb.'

Najwa Zebian

The shaking didn't stop for hours. The café heaved with police and ADT security guards and hysteria and Goodwin Chiyangwa answered questions and answered them again and still his hands – would – not – be – still.

His mind kept downloading clips that flashed and receded.

'Yes I just put their food down – chicken wraps – the two women and the one had the baby, yes. And then – ' (He was rambling. Did he think the officer cared if it was chicken wraps?)

Part of the movie played again. Flashed and receded. Flashed and receded.

Another coffee yes sho' coming right up.

He turns and sees them. Sickening sweat of realisation.

Down down down get down.

He hits the floor – screams – sobs of fear.

The baby.

Coffee drips hot on his neck.

It's ok ma'am. Ok. It's ok.

He inches his body closer. The baby sleeps.

It's so *not ok.*

Famous – the security guard who'd made that stretch of Victoria Road his beat – he'd been watching cars. Posing and laughing and charming tourists in his yellow hi-vis vest. Wedged as he was under the table and facing the street, Goodwin had seen it all. He'd seen Famous seeing the gunmen seeing that they'd been seen. They were edgy and unhinged. It wasn't rush hour at Trend but even for brazen armed robbers this was a stupid time of day for a heist.

More questions from the officer.

'I don't know, maybe Mozambican. I'm from Zim. Not sure, boss.'

They'd screamed at Famous even as he was screaming for the police.

'Then the one with the gun,' Goodwin stumbled on through the strange juddering of his recall, 'Well they all had guns but that one guy – he aimed at the security guard and he shot – but the girl there – ' he pointed to where the white girl had been sitting – she came often and he liked her a lot and now her blood –

He'd seen her reach up from under the table – her phone? It was as if the men hadn't noticed her – and then the shot –

She'd crumpled like a dry shirt suddenly unpegged from a wash line.

'Thanks man. I think that's it for now then.' The officer gave Goodwin an awkward pat on the shoulder then busied himself on his phone.

Goodwin's boss, Adrian, appeared from the kitchen. He was always white but today he was *seriously* white.

'Goodwin – could you – I dunno – maybe just – '

'Sho' boss.'

Adrian had been rendered utterly decision-less. Goodwin had seen others like this, in the aftermath of trauma. Unable to decide. Unable to do.

So he started doing. He autopiloted himself into doing the next right thing, and then the next right thing, and the choice steadied him, breaking over him in waves like the waves that hadn't stopped breaking on the beach across the road even as the girl was shot.

Next right thing. Next right thing.

He picked up broken glass and a butter knife flung under a table. Straightened chairs. He made his way out onto the deck where the young white woman had been. A generous tipper. Always kind and smiling. Sometimes she came with that guy and sometimes – like today – she came alone.

He doubted she'd ever come again.

The police had taken all the evidence they needed and Ivy who normally worked in the kitchen was mopping. Mopping and sobbing and shaking as the water turned red. So much blood. *So much blood.* Goodwin shuddered and tried to keep going. Stacked chairs. Picked up a half glass of flat Sprite where the girl had sat, the ice long melted.

And her Bible. It was open – blood spatters – in the book of Isaiah.

Goodwin's face went suddenly numb.

What do I do? What do I do? What do I do?

Ivy was sobbing harder. Instinctively he snapped shut the Bible – smooth, brown, faux leather cover – because he didn't want Ivy seeing any more of the trauma – any more of the dry dark lifeless blood – and he slid the Bible into the marsupial pouch of his Trend apron and then he did the next right thing, and then the next right thing.

The sun was low when Adrian finally gathered the staff, haltingly thanked them and said he'd be in touch in the morning.

'The cops will let us know but let's aim for an 11am start? I think

27

everything's – you know – more or less – cleaned up.' Adrian swept a hand across his forehead – through his hair – fighting tears.

By the time Goodwin stumbled back into his street in Woodstock – walk-taxi-walk – it was dark. He knew every corner store, every pavement crack, every beggar and blocked drain.

When he first came to South Africa he stayed in Khayelitsha with a cousin's friend, Kutenda, a fellow Zimbo who'd promised – and delivered – a foreigner's education on How To Make It In Cape Town. Everything from airtime and employment agencies to xenophobia and where to buy cheap *zamalek*.

A Geography teacher in Zimbabwe, Goodwin thought he'd try for gardening work in Cape Town's southern suburbs. If he couldn't get a post teaching – and he couldn't – keeping his hands in the soil was at least something.

But three months into turning flowerbeds and mowing immaculate, shaded lawns, he knew he had to find something else. He was sending almost all his earnings back to Zim via EcoCash, to his mom and his sister, Aneni. Transport was eating everything else, and he was eating almost nothing.

Kutenda came through for him again – knew a guy who knew a guy who was hiring waiters and baristas.

Kutenda texted Goodwin with laughing emojis –

How hard can it be?

Not hard at all, Goodwin decided, something almost like hope daring to sputter. He'd caught a taxi to Camps Bay, convinced Adrian he was a quick learner, left the world of white people's gardens and discovered the magic of the coffee bean.

Not long after landing the job at Trend, he and Kutenda moved out of the shack they'd shared in Khayelitsha. Spaza shops run by Somalis and Nigerians were being looted, burned or worse every week in the townships and squatter camps of Cape Town. Goodwin and Kutenda both had valid work permits but still, guys like them were *kwerekwere* – foreigners – and unwelcome.

Woodstock was a melting pot of transvestites, illegal immigrants, do-gooder whites trying to bridge gaps, coloureds, Xhosas, Indian spice and all things nice and not so nice. They found a one-bedroom flat to rent, and things were better. Their landlady was a large, bustling, coloured woman named Frieda. She insisted on speaking to Goodwin and Kutenda in rapid Afrikaans, to which they nodded submissively, and gradually became more adept at interpreting her rules and rantings by tone, body language and animated gesticulations.

Goodwin knew his mom prayed for him every day. She prayed for his safety and his happiness and a stable job. She prayed he'd keep sending money home and eventually send himself once again and meet a nice girl and settle down.

Goodwin prayed less and less. The xenophobia had gotten under his skin which was just as black as the skin of those who lurched in doorways and spat or threw beer bottles in his direction. And though his default demeanour of phlegmatic gentleness would never let on, he was angry. Angry at Mugabe for ruining his homeland and forcing him to head south. Angry at South Africa for holding him at arms' length when he had every legal right to be here. Angry at God for letting African history unravel the way it inevitably did.

And after today. *After today?* He had no inclination to cling to his tenuous faith at all.

He felt strange – un-tethered – climbing the stairs of the apartment block.

'*Wena*, why you still wearing your apron?' It was Buhle. A tiny, skinny, wisp of a beautiful thing. Eight or nine years old. She lived with her aunt and cousins in the flat above. She hovered on the stairs, grinning up at Goodwin as if she'd stolen something sweet.

'Eh?' Goodwin was dead on his feet. 'What now, *sisi*?

'You still serving coffee, *wena*,' she giggled. He looked down at himself as if from a very great height. His apron was splattered with coffee and something that *was not coffee* and he shuddered as images again flashed and receded.

'*Eish*, I can't believe,' he faked a smile – patted Buhle on the head – fumbled with keys – Kutenda was out – closed the door behind him.

Stood still in the dark. Willed the shaking to stop.

He flicked on a light. Slowly lifted the apron overhead. Slung it over –

Something heavy thudded against the chair back.

Then an exhausted thought: *The girl's Bible.*

Whether it was shock or grief or fear or wild desperation to believe that life was worth the living –

Goodwin slumped into the chair –

Opened the book.

Pages flopped and settled.

Something was highlighted in girlish purple. John sixteen, verse thirty-three.

'I have told you all this so that you may have peace in Me. Here on earth you will have many trials and sorrows. But take heart, because I have overcome the world.'

The shaking gave way to consuming convulsions. Goodwin rested his head on the words and wept.

4

Pretoria

'We all mould one another's dreams. We all hold each other's fragile hopes in our hands.'

Anonymous

JD wasn't JD's *actual* name. His *actual* name was Joshua Dean du Preez. But JD was easier to say and spell. Also, you weren't supposed to pronounce the 'z' at the end of his surname which made him shouty and punchy sometimes because people *did* pronounce it and what was the point *anyway* of putting it there then? It made him feel conspicuous – like the name didn't fit properly.

Nothing seemed to fit properly today. He knew his mom was doing silent-crying which she thought he couldn't see but he always could. He wasn't exactly sure what dyslexia was. (*Dislipsia? Dyslazyeye?*) But it had to do with why the teachers pretended to like him but actually didn't and why he aggressively loathed homework and why he pretended to read while words dived and swam like so many black dolphins across oceans of pages.

It was what that lady had just discussed with them in kind, patronizing tones – pointing to the damning graphs and figures of some sort of test that JD must've undergone without realising it was a test because if he'd known it was a test he would've gone hot then cold then stupid.

He felt sick. He didn't care if he had distazergun but he hated that it made his mom sad and even though it was *his* problem not *hers* because *he* was the one who had to get through the dumb book about some lion and a witch and kids in a cupboard – he got that it was very much her problem too and he hated himself for doing whatever he did to allow the dyslegalize germ to get into his brain and destroy things.

Lizette could barely see the black blur of tar as rain chased across the windscreen and the wipers kept up their useless frantic beat. *So this – this haze – this is what it's like for him, trying to read,* she thought, glancing at her ten-year-old son in the passenger seat beside her. The highveld thunderstorm held a cosmic mirror to their lives, reflecting the diagnosis that had just flooded their reality.

Above the weary thwack-thwack of the wipers the radio blurted the dramatic jingle of 702's Eyewitness News. An armed robbery at a café in Cape Town. Woman shot. Critical.

'Witnesses say – '

Lizette flicked off the radio. Other people's pain was too much for her right now thank you very much. They just needed to get home.

Home.

It was only just starting to feel like that.

Lizette had fallen pregnant in her second year of varsity. A combination of alcohol, insecurity, and the varsity's annual Spring Day revelries. It wasn't rape, exactly. Or was it? Consensus or coercion? The question had tormented her for a decade.

She regretted it the moment it was over. She pretended to have her life together. She accepted the consequences. She loved her son. She wallowed in shame. She finished her degree. She lived with her parents. She got back on her feet. She got a job as PA to the HR Manager of Netcare Pretoria East Hospital. She loved her work. She loved her colleagues. She slaved and saved to put JD into a small private school. She got off at three-thirty to fetch him after sports. She joined a church.

They passed it now – the lit sign on the building a smudge of light in the rain. *Hope Church* – the 'H' made to look kind of like a cross. The plot of land on which the church was built had been donated by a magnanimous billionaire a decade ago and the grounds were magnificent. Verdant lawns were shaded by enormous jacarandas and because the church was within walking distance from their townhouse complex, Lizette would sometimes bring JD to ride his bike between the trees on Saturday afternoons.

Nearly home, she thought.

Hope Church was a big, cool, contemporary, interdenominational church with bands and baristas and skinny jeans and tattoos and it seemed they were singing the latest Hillsong releases before they were released.

But it went deeper than cool.

In the throes of her unplanned pregnancy and driven by guilt and shame, she'd compulsively visited about a dozen churches. Conservative, big-stick, Bible-thumping churches where foot-tapping was frowned upon, never mind raising a hand. And liberal, anything-goes, slain-in-the-Spirit churches where you were expected to fall over in a babbling mess on the carpet. Despite all this, somewhere – somehow – sometime between potty-training and lunchbox-packing – God had gripped her heart and upended her life with the peace of Christ.

Hope Church had surprised her. It was different. The doctrinal pendulum didn't swing wildly out of whack in the direction of either legalism or licentiousness. A team of preachers and leaders shared the pulpit, unapologetically expounding the truth of Scripture without leaving out the politically incorrect bits. And people seemed to worship freely, authentically, emotionally – like it was a whole-body experience.

On her second or third Sunday at Hope Church, the preacher had said,

'The more conservative our theology is? The more liberal our loving should be.' Lizette's own pendulum had settled dead centre along that plumb line of truth. She stayed.

Not that she didn't still have to scrape together all her bits of brave to go to church each week, where she felt obliged to down a social potion that was equal parts judgment and pity – real or perceived – handed to her by perfect women adorning the arms of perfect men and trailed by perfect kids dressed in brands. She couldn't attend morning moms' meetings because, *duh, some women work* so she missed out on the mom-type small-talk that inevitably built the kind of comfortable familiarity that potentially bloomed into friendship. But still, Hope was the closest thing to a spiritual home she'd ever known. She welcomed the weight of safety it offered her – the space to worship more or less anonymously on a Sunday.

She was through the complex gates now. Into the carport – dash through the rain – quick wiping of tears. JD dumped his school bag in front of the TV, an unsubtle declaration of how he planned to escape homework.

'Lunchbox to the sink, boy.'

'Ok.'

It's unlikely that he will cope with mainstream schooling.

The ed psych's recommendations tore up her mind like bombs dropped. The words whirled and dizzied her.

Home-schooling? Tutoring? Private tuition? That's like, paying someone's salary, came her horrified thought.

She knew her parents would try to help if she asked them but could they really afford to dip any deeper into a dwindling pension fund and could she expect them to keep working for another ten years because that's what it would take and was there a chance the tests were wrong and it wasn't that bad but if it *was* that bad could she really pick up any extra hours at work and revise her already questionable definition of 'coping'?

Mechanically she rinsed JD's lunchbox. Though distorted by rain thrashing against the glass, the Hope Church sign was still just visible from the kitchen window. Normally, she liked it. Today it felt like a cruel joke because, where was the hope now? Where was God?

July
2 0 1 5

'Now, with God's help, I shall become myself.'

Søren Kierkegaard

5

Istanbul

'I am become a name;
For always roaming with a hungry heart
Much have I seen and known; cities of men
And manners, climates, councils, governments,
Myself not least...'

Alfred, Lord Tennyson

Drew Hamilton-Brown's phone had been off for weeks. There hadn't been much reception in Kathmandu and even less chance of plugging in a charger, so he'd switched it off altogether, glad of the escape.

The irony of his escape wasn't lost on him as he worked tirelessly to help those whose health and homes had *not* escaped the earthquake of April 25th.

It was the earthquake that had offered him this plausible, admirable escape. He'd arrived in Nepal in June. Two months after the tragedy, non-profits Direct Relief and Global Giving still had a strong presence in the country. They needed hands to drive and deliver and clean and care as they initiated or supported longer-term recovery efforts, and he'd gladly given himself over to the buzz of humanitarian aid which at least for a while drowned out the voices in his head making snide remarks about his lack of purpose.

He felt desperate for the Nepalese. The devastation of landscape and livelihoods – the fragility of a here-today-gone-tomorrow life – left him cold despite the stifling humidity. But when all was said and done, Kathmandu had been little more than another distraction. Another thing to do. Another place to go. Another escape.

Thematically, 'escape' summed up this long, insouciant chapter of Drew's life. But today, in a tea shop off Istanbul's Grand Bazaar, he'd dredged up the resolve to be responsible. Bought data. Switched on his phone.

Texts began pinging through, pulling him back to the reality of everything he was running from.

Drew had finished his architecture degree at Wits University in Johannesburg, done a TEFL course which set him up to teach English anywhere, hugged his mom at international departures of O.R. Tambo, and left.

In less than two years and in no particular order he'd been to Egypt, Morocco, Spain, Botswana, Namibia, Zambia, Mozambique, Réunion (a month he didn't remember, on account of being very high for extended periods of time), Zanzibar and Thailand. Then Nepal. Now Turkey.

He sighed, slumped in his grubby plastic chair, and glanced at his phone. Mom.

Hello boy. Miss you. Think of you and pray for you every day. It would be wonderful to know if you're alive? Just saying.

(With many, *many* happy emojis interspersed.)

His mom had always stressed the importance of tone, and her texting left no room for misinterpretation. He smiled now at her thinly veiled attempts to control her need to be in control. He knew how hard it had been for her to let out the kite strings and watch him fly free. Not hard. It was killing her. And it didn't help that he was rubbish at contacting her with proof of life. The text went on –

Can you believe the jasmine buds are turning pink and it's only July! Global warming I tell you. Shannon's kids come round most days because they know I'm baking for the church fête. Sweet things. (The kids, not the things I'm making. Savoury tarts.)

Neighbour kids, thought Drew. *Poor mom.* He pushed the terrifying thought (of the grandkids his mom badly wanted) immediately from his mind – left it squarely at the feet of Stella, his older, married sister – and read on.

He knew his mom was lonely, and though he'd never say it out loud he was amazed at how she continuously made meaning: filling her life by pouring it out on others. She happily, stubbornly maintained, as Mariane Pearl had, that self-pity, even if legitimate, never fails to sap your strength. That simple, difficult mindset engendered her with incredible capacity to be cheerful despite circumstances.

A few years ago, she'd roped Drew into helping at a church women's event. Thinking back, there may have been bribery of sorts. He was tasked with carrying urns from the kitchen to the courtyard of St Simon's Anglican Church where his mom was a pillar of prayer and practical involvement and where he had resentfully attended Sunday School for most of his childhood.

His mom was 'doing the talk' that day, as she put it. For some reason he remembered the flyer. *Worship while you wait – a word from Helen Hamilton-Brown.* He felt awkward and out of place amidst the mostly ancient ladies in compression stockings and Green Cross shoes (the ugly kind, not the trendy kind). There were scones with Marmite and grated cheese and he knew the tea would be lukewarm by the time they served it and it all felt like something from the seventies and he was miffed with his mom for being so committed to this community.

Her lilting voice had carried across the courtyard in microphoned gusts as he relayed the finger-burning urns across gravel and grass and he remembered the words now as he flicked through texts at this sticky pavement table more than ten thousand kilometres from home. She'd said, 'Using our spiritual gifts is the best way out of hopelessness. Ladies, we've got to praise God in the waiting.'

He remembered his irritation. *Cheesy Christian-esy.*

Now he thought: *What's she waiting for? Heaven? A husband?*

He couldn't deny the older he got, the more he worried about her.

A text from his dad.

Hey Drew. Happy Birthday. Dad.

Drew had turned twenty-five a month before. Another evening in Kathmandu he couldn't recall with much clarity. He didn't bother to check when the message had been sent but for sure his dad would've forgotten on the day. He was on Wife Number Three – *Miranda? Melinda?* – and living in Brisbane.

At first Drew had felt faintly guilty that his dad's bottomless Australian credit card was paying for his life. But he got over it. He did earn reasonable money now and then, teaching English online. He wasn't a *total* freeloader. And he knew the limitless cash supply was more about appeasing his dad's guilt for excusing himself – politely and permanently – from Drew's life. So really, he was doing his old man a bit of a favour.

Another text. From Allie, Kayla's mom. Drew caught his breath.

Oh crap I'm such a bad person.

He'd hardly contacted the family since hearing about the shooting. Again, to escape. He and Kayla had been at primary school together, before going their separate ways to an all-boys and all-girls, respectively, Anglican high school. Their families had hung out a lot before his parents' divorce. He was intimidated by her diehard faith – which he didn't share, and she knew it – but she really was a special friend. On the plane from Nepal he'd started reading *Sophie's Choice* by William Styron and a line came to him now –

'There are friends one makes at a youthful age in whom one simply rejoices, for whom one possesses a love and loyalty mysteriously lacking in the friendships made in after-years, no matter how genuine.'

Kayla was just that, to Drew. And he didn't want to face the fear, and the rage. Because how was it *possible* that this could have happened to one of the nicest people ever?

Allie had added Drew to a massive WhatsApp group – the infuriating kind where every other human on the group feels the compulsion to send a plethora of praying-hands emojis. He scrolled up. Months of messages skimmed by –

Hi friends and fam – thank you so much for your prayers. Kayla is still in ICU. Doc says she's not out of the woods, though we thank God she's stable.

Thank God? Thank God she was shot through the womb and she might not make it and if she doesn't die she will definitely never have kids and maybe that will make her wish she had died?

Drew realised he hadn't been breathing while scanning the texts about Kayla. He let out a shaky breath and his phone dropped to the table. Memories surfaced. Playing Marco Polo in the Rays' swimming pool on hot December days. Kayla shone a light on his wild life that simultaneously annoyed him and made him feel awkward and guilty and strangely appreciative. He'd always had a soft spot for her. Always would.

Drew paid for his tea and wandered towards the mess, noise and colour of the Grand Bazaar, his thoughts about Kayla turning to the carpet vendors, the leather jacket touts, the women selling pastries and pistachios.

And also, if Jesus is supposed to be the big answer to everything, then all these Muslims are going to hell and how can that be fair?

The aggressive market bargaining going on all around him matched and validated the anger building in him, even as he acknowledged the irony of being angry at Someone he wasn't sure existed.

Unbidden, another memory. Mrs Gregory. Tiny, old, delicate. His Grade 3 teacher. She used to call Drew to her desk when he was boisterous – belligerent – out of sorts. She'd say, 'Drew. Who is behind Mr Angry? I don't want to talk to Mr Angry. I want to talk to the person standing *behind* Mr Angry.' Hot coursing tears. And Fear had stepped out, sheepish. Fear of his dad's shouting and disdain. Fear of rejection and abandonment.

Was it fear now, he wondered, making him mad? He supposed there was fear. He feared Kayla wouldn't pull through. And there was something closer to despair – the kind he'd seen on faces of mothers in Kathmandu.

Absentmindedly Drew fingered the deep soft pile of a carpet, oblivious to the eager sales pitch of the seller. Resignation settled on his soul, making him feel grown up and wise and honest.

He realised how desperately he wanted God to exist – the way this carpet existed in all its real, obvious, tangible *there*-ness. He desperately wanted to believe in a God big enough to handle his anger. He desperately wanted to believe there was more to life than this.

He just knew he never could.

6

Durban

'The aim of life is to live, and to live means to be aware, joyously, drunkenly, serenely, divinely aware.'

Henry Miller

Find your freedom.

Jules McIntosh glanced at the lavender fields lit by the photoshopped French sunset on the cover of the magazine. Bryce often nabbed inflight literature and brought it home for her. It was his sweet way of letting her know she was never far from his thoughts, even as he commuted to Joburg or London to meet with clients in frequent flyer lounges or in cafés in Sandton or Canary Wharf.

This was an old mag – summer of 2014 – but she'd kept it on her bedside table because for some reason those lavender fields – such perfect, peaceful rows! – kept hope alive.

Maybe one day, she thought.

At thirty-seven, travelling was part of a life Jules had broken up with and it didn't look like they were ever getting back together. These days, the height of adventure was picnicking on the trampoline with the three small humans she was raising, or performing Electrolux ballet during which she pirouetted elegantly around the vacuum cleaner for her cheering toddlers while sucking up dog hairs in the lounge, careful not to trip on the cord.

She felt ridiculous, living vicariously through the cover of an airline magazine. She loved her life, after all. She and her family lacked for nothing and not a day passed when she wasn't acutely grateful for her beautiful Mia, David and Leila. Her incredible Bryce. Their old-home-fixed-up in Glen Ashley.

But every decision involves a sacrifice. The decision she'd made was not to use her Information Design degree – ever, really – and to be a stay-at-home mom instead – and the sacrifice was the Something Big she wanted to do with her life.

Not that being a mom isn't *Something Big*, went the seesaw of her self-recriminatory thoughts. And not that she really had a clear idea of what the Something Big was. Maybe the bone-weary exhaustion she lived with was just a God-tug towards Something Big that didn't exist earth-side. Something *Bigger*. Eternity.

But still.

Bryce was a financial advisor – setting people up to leave fiscal legacies to future generations – and the most exciting part of her day was mostly when *oh my word mayonnaise is on special I'm going to buy three and put two on the shelf for next month!*

The paradox was that, even without Something Big, her life was so full and frenetic that sometimes she couldn't think. Couldn't breathe. She didn't remember ever intentionally choosing to be thrust body and soul into the cake sales, play dates and parking lot politics of preschool life, the hosting and volunteering of church life, the relentless cooking, cleaning, shopping and organising of momming and wifing. Somehow, a life had taken shape around her. She was responsible for keeping that life afloat, as well as the lives of her loved ones.

When will I ever stop treading water? she wondered. *How did all this stuff get piled on my plate?* she thought. And then, because images of laden plates treading water rankled the grammar sheriff in her: *When did it become ok to mix my metaphors?*

Yet, there were moments. Exquisite moments when she deeply felt the quiddity of her life.

Moments when David would be teetering gleefully on the edge of a jungle gym – a superhero universe of his own imagining – and she would caution, 'Be careful!' and he would vehemently, obstinately reply, 'I *am* becarefulling!' Moments when Mia – five and fearless – would put a hand in hers and ask for help. Moments when Jules would rock and shush her littlest baby Leila in the night, feeling – closer than breathing – the presence of the God who made her babies and a million stars hanging silent as she glanced skyward through bedroom blinds.

And moments like this.

Bryce emerged from their en suite bathroom freshly showered and towel wrapped. He smelled amazing.

He flopped onto the bed next to Jules.

'You ok?' he asked.

'I guess.' She knew her smile was unconvincing.

He turned towards her. 'You are extremely pretty,' he said seriously, as if he'd been conducting research and was now divulging his findings. 'And outrageously sexy.'

She laughed, despite the big dark thoughts that marinated in the disquiet of her mind about her self-worth and the point of it all. She was so grateful for the way he loved her. Even when they were dating, Bryce had intuitively understood the fragility just beneath the layers of her chin-up, get-it-done, don't-be-pathetic demeanour.

There'd been a night when she was fourteen. Her parents had had friends round for dinner. She'd been out of sight, out of mind, busy with homework and appearing only when it was absolutely necessary to be polite.

But she'd overheard most of the conversation.

'Jules is turning into quite a beauty!' This from the woman. Jules couldn't even remember who the people were.

'Yip,' her mom had said. Jules had heard the third G and T in her voice. 'She's got a face that turns heads. And a body that doesn't.'

Laughter. All of them, laughing. Because she was *fat*.

And that was that. The shame had fixed itself to her life – cloyingly, like wet, embarrassing clothes one-size-too-small – and she knew she'd never be free.

Except, Bryce.

Bryce – tall, charming, clever, funny Bryce – saw her six years later in a university cafeteria. He saw her intense green eyes and the splash of freckles across cheeks that bracketed a perfect smile. He saw her quick mind and her easy laugh. And where she saw her too-big reflection in the mirror, he saw voluptuous wonder.

'Gee thanks,' she said to him now, lacing her fingers through his. 'I just – I don't know – I guess lately I'm feeling like my get-up-and-go might have got up and left. Like, I kind of wish I had some amazing change-the-world qualities. Like Beth.'

Beth was a petite, effervescent brunette, a worship leader who was also dominating the Christian speaking circuit. A prolific songwriter, she had a couple of albums to her name and some record-breaking Spotify downloads. She was a fellow mom at Mia's preschool and she and Jules had struck up a bit of a friendship despite how much she intimidated Jules, who couldn't believe a woman like that ever had fat days, or lonely days, or not-good-enough days.

Bryce looked at her, all mock seriousness gone. Real seriousness in its place.

'Oh babe. Beth-shmeth. Forget Beth. I mean, what is she, Bible Barbie?' Jules gave him The Look. 'Ok ok, that's mean. I like her. I really do. But what are *you* passionate about? Like, really passionate? Besides me obviously.' (Mock seriousness back again.)

Hardly thinking – tears almost welling – Jules blurted –

'Litter.'

'Litter?'

'Yes, litter. I know it's stupid but I think about it all the time. How different life would be – the world would be – if people just freaking used dustbins! I fantasize about it, Bryce. I know how crazy that sounds. But I do. I fantasize about starting massive anti-litter campaigns and cleaning up the world and having neat pavements and I just know it will make people nicer and less likely to yell in the traffic or beat their wives or – I don't know – like that New York mayor – remember? – and the subways – and there was less crime – '

She stopped. Emotional and embarrassed and thinking, *Did I just verbalise the Something Big?*

Bryce didn't laugh. Another thing she loved about him. He never laughed at her wild ideas, the ones that worked and the ones that didn't.

'What you're passionate about,' he said softly, 'it's the very first thing God charged us with. You know, look after the planet and all that. I think it's brilliant Jules. I think we should go for it.'

She grinned. 'Go for it? But – '

'What's more,' Bryce added, 'I see your amazing, change-the-world qualities.'

'Wow. Really? Like, *both* of them?' She gave him a sideways smile –

sarcasm and self-deprecation not so easily dislodged from her arsenal of self-preservation.

Undaunted, Bryce continued, 'Of course, you have *lots* of amazing, change-the-world qualities. But right now I'm particularly focused on the qualities beneath your pyjamas, which I find not only very distracting, but also, very distracting.'

He flicked off the bedside lamp. And happily, marvellously, just for a moment, Jules stopped treading water, laid down her laden plate of life, and gave herself over to the refuge of love-making because maybe somewhere, somehow, everything was going to be alright.

7

Pretoria

'All that is gold does not glitter,
Not all those who wander are lost;
The old that is strong does not wither,
Deep roots are not reached by the frost.

From the ashes a fire shall be woken,
A light from the shadows shall spring;
Renewed shall be blade that was broken,
The crownless again shall be king.'

J.R.R. Tolkien

The only thing JD (kind of) looked forward to about church was bashing around on the drums in the King's Kids hall before the other boys got herded in, amped and sweaty from playing touch rugby, and the girls broke out of their clusters of giggles and took seats.

JD was so-so at sport. He didn't mind chasing a ball if there was nothing else to do. But he didn't fit the jock profile so he was always last-pick and no one passed to him so instead he thumped the bass pedal and whacked the crash cymbal with all the pent up frustration of someone pretending none of it mattered.

'Hey JD.'

It was Nadia: eyes bright, glad to see him, younger than his mom, just as beautiful. She was one of the King's Kids leaders.

JD struggled to read but he didn't struggle to be honest, with others and himself, and he thought again now that he liked Nadia *so* much, even though he wasn't totally into girls yet. The leaders were on a roster, which meant he only got Nadia as group leader every third week or so. And those weeks were *the best.*

His mom kept saying how she wished JD had more male role models. Father figures. She was always agreeing to outdoorsy days with other families, even though he knew it sucked for her to be the single mom with no husband to carry the folding chairs and the cooler box. He also knew she was right. He knew there were things that *clicked* when a man explained them to him. But, although he didn't know all the guy leaders at King's Kids, those he did know seemed kind of flaky. Again, he couldn't read words well, but he could read people. He knew when someone was forcing or faking or just saying what they knew people expected.

Nadia was different. She was for real. He knew the colours of her insides matched the colours of her outsides.

And she understood. She never made JD read aloud from the Bible. Instead she got him to make sound effects for whatever story she was telling. A lesson or two in, she realised he had rhythm. So when David said to Goliath, *'You come to me with sword, spear, and javelin, but I come to you in the name of the LORD of Heaven's Armies – the God of the armies of Israel, whom you have defied,'* JD would be the beat box of suspense just before the stones were flung into the giant's forehead.

He would lose himself in the timbre of Nadia's voice, forgetting how the other kids seemed smarter and how he was always catching up on the missed beats of written words the way he never missed a beat on drums.

'Are you guys heading somewhere straight after church?' Nadia asked.

'Don't think so. Why?'

'Reuben is keen to meet you. He'd like you to have a go on his drums.' She made it sound like JD would be doing this guy a favour. She was *so* cool. Reuben was her boyfriend – a drummer in the church worship band.

'Ok awesome,' he smiled at her. 'Thanks.'

Then for an hour he didn't hear a word. His thoughts went *drums drums drums I get to play drums drums drums!* And finally *amen at last it's done let's get outta here!*

'Let's get outta here,' laughed Nadia as if she could see right inside his brain. He walked next to her across the lawn towards the main church building feeling shy and cool and happy. He waved at his mom and shouted something about *quickly-looking-at-drums-see-you-now!* She was hovering amongst a group of women with prams, sipping a frothy coffee he knew she didn't want because she only really liked tea at night just before bed. He'd asked her once why she drank coffee at church anyway and she'd told him it was easier to talk to the other moms if she had something to hold and pretend to be busy with and he suddenly wondered if his mom would like a Reuben of her own to date and introduce to people.

They were at the front of the church now. Reuben leapt down from the stage – crazy blonde hair – ripped jeans – and grabbed JD in half-a-hug, half-a-handshake and said 'What's up, bro?' like JD was his homey, but it didn't feel flaky or fake. Just friendly. Then he gave Nadia a (long) kiss and they looked into each other's eyes and JD looked at the floor.

'Hey so I'm so keen to hear you play, dude,' enthused Reuben when the looking-into-eyes part was finally over. 'Nadia says you're a legend with the sticks! C'mon, let's hear you, man!'

JD couldn't wipe the smile off his face even though he was trying to be cool and he wondered if his mom would let him rip holes in his jeans. They were new from Mr Price so he doubted it but it was worth a shot. He hopped on stage and settled in behind the Pearl kit. Reuben handed over his sticks.

'Should I – like – ' JD stammered self-consciously.

'Go for it.' Reuben was grinning and JD thought if Chandler Bing from *Friends* (which he wasn't supposed to watch) was here, he would say to Reuben, 'Could you *be* more chilled out?'

JD played. Hard and loud and with all the energy and attention he couldn't level at books.

Then he stopped, still grinning. Shushed the cymbals.

'Cool,' he said, for want of anything more eloquent. The church had mostly emptied out. Nadia was chatting to an older woman halfway down the aisle.

'Cool?' said Reuben. 'Dude, you're way cooler than cool! You've got an incredible sound. I'd be stoked if you ever wanted to hang out. No charge. I'm not a pro but I've probably got some tips to get you up to, like, gig standards.'

Gigs?

The door to a world of possibility turned slowly on the hinges of JD's mind. Reuben was watching him. Then he said, 'JD. When you play – what do you feel?'

Without thinking –

'Like I can breathe. Like I'm free.'

Reuben smiled but JD saw he had actual *tears* in his eyes. Adults were so weird.

'Not to be weird or anything, bro – ' again, with the mind-reading! 'But I think that's God.'

'Huh?' said JD, though he kinda-sorta knew what Reuben meant because he had kinda-sorta suspected it really was God who made him able to play and he wasn't so bored or confused or cross about God when he was drumming. In fact, when he was drumming, he thought God was nice.

'Well, we sing that stuff, right? About God being the air we breathe and the breath in our lungs? The name God calls Himself in the Bible – *Yahweh* – it's pronounced like the same sound we make breathing in, and breathing out. So it's like, the first and last thing each of us will ever say.'

JD sucked in air and stared at Reuben. *Woah. Far out.*

'And *freedom* – that's the essence of the gospel,' Reuben continued, and JD thought, *This guy is more than a drummer.* 'We get it so messed up half the time. We think Christianity is about God taking bad people and making them good. But it's more than that – better than that. He's all about taking trapped people and setting them free – setting *us* free – and *keeping* us free. Free from sin. Free to pursue His purposes for us. And I think – when you play the drums – you get it. I think it's part of your purpose – like, your calling.'

JD was staring at Reuben and fighting the prick at the back of his eyes – determined not to be weird like a grownup.

Don't cry don't cry don't cry.

'Sorry dude,' Reuben went on, 'I'm going totally preacher on you! I just feel like I really need to tell you, man: God knows your name.'

JD dropped the sticks – clutched his face – an involuntary reflex to stop or hide or surrender to – he wasn't sure which – the spilling tears. Reuben was at his side. He didn't say anything more. He couldn't really, on account of JD's heaving sobs, which told Reuben all he needed to know about the pain of being a mistake. The pain of being misunderstood, and a misfit. The pain of not belonging, which had led to not believing. He crouched next to JD and let the boy's pain leak away.

Slowly JD caught his breath. Tried to laugh – embarrassed – and lifted his shirt to his eyes.

Did God *really* know his name? Would He call him JD, or Joshua Dean, or something else entirely? Did God know his mom's name too?

Oh no. Mom.

He'd been crying and she would know and that would make her cry too and he didn't want her crying because he badly wanted her *also* to breathe, and feel free.

And he was the reason she couldn't.

8

Johannesburg

'There are only two ways to live your life. One is as though nothing is a miracle. The other is as though everything is a miracle.'

Albert Einstein

For Goodwin, there was nothing quite like the comfortable aroma of bacon, hot butter, coffee and conversation. It helped him believe in good people. A good world. Even a good God.

He breathed in the hiss of steaming milk – poured out the leaves of another perfect fern – art in another cardboard cup – scrawled another name – smiled and fuelled another human's day with caffeine.

It was surreal – how things were the same and yet so different, in this Trend café.

His whole-world-switch-up had transpired in what seemed like a heartbeat – less than a month ago.

Adrian had asked Goodwin to meet him early one Monday morning, before his shift in Camps Bay. It happened to be the Monday that came after the Sunday night Kutenda had arrived home to their Woodstock flat, bleeding.

Kutenda had gone back to Khayelitsha to visit a friend. He'd stopped at a spaza shop to buy airtime. The shop was run by Somalis and had been broken into three times. The Somalis knew it was xenophobic locals, trying to sink immigrant businesses. They knew from witnesses that one of the perpetrators wore a blue Nike sweater. They knew he'd come back. The *tsotsis* always did, to gloat. The Somalis were mad. And ready.

Kutenda had sauntered up to the counter – smiled – and put down R50. 'Vodacom please.' He was wearing a blue Nike sweater. It was an Oxfam relic he'd picked up years ago in Harare. Had not another Zimbabwean been in the shop at the time, and had he not heard Kutenda's torrent of anguished Shona as the Somalis rained blows on his head, and had he not screamed at them to stop – Kutenda would have died.

The next day, at Adrian's request, Goodwin had arrived at Trend at 6am, half an hour before the first customers would hurry in for crack-of-dawn coffees and pre-work business meetings. Normally, at this time of morning, Goodwin would drink in the roaring orchestra of the waves, unrivalled by traffic. That morning, he didn't even glance seaward. He knocked lightly on the glass door. Adrian came through from the kitchen, unlocked, and ushered Goodwin in from the frigid, dark, June morning.

Adrian stared. It took him a moment, then –

'Goodwin! What the – ? What's happened?'

Goodwin tried a sheepish smile, willing himself to perk up. The Trend staff had recovered – sort of – from the November shooting, but Kutenda's muffled sobs at the kitchen counter the night before while Goodwin swabbed Dettol into the wounds had reminded him that his own wounds needed staunching still.

He told Adrian about Kutenda and the spaza shop, the sweater, the Somalis, the blood.

'So anyway, I don't know, boss, these guys…' He shook his head and pretended to be laughing off the madness of senseless violence, like, *whatever, the world's a crazy place.*

'Flip. I'm so sorry, man. I'm so sorry,' Adrian repeated, his whole body alive with flustered consternation. 'It just sucks so badly! I hate that you guys go through this stuff. But actually,' he sighed, 'maybe this makes a difference to what I want to talk to you about. What's keeping you in Cape Town? I mean, besides this job?'

The question surprised Goodwin. 'Eh – not much, I guess? Kutenda. One or two friends. Why boss?'

'The manager of Trend at O.R. Tambo was caught with his fingers in the till last week. Literally. The guy's been siphoning cash for months. Drug habit. So they fired his sorry arse.'

'Wow. So much good news today, boss,' Goodwin chuckled despite himself. 'But what does it have to do with us?'

'Well, it has something to do with *you*. Head office called me for recommendations. I told them if they offer you the job I'll be furious. And they'd be stupid not to.'

'But – me? What, *manager*? Joburg?' Goodwin found himself grinning. Adrian looked relieved.

'Dude, I don't want to lose you, you know that right? You're the best I've got. And I'd rather chew broken glass than train another new freakin' barista, for flip's sake! But you know as well as I do, you're too bright to be making coffees all your life. You can go places.'

Like most big decisions Goodwin had made, it took him a matter of seconds to know what he'd choose. He always went with his gut:

Dread or excitement?

Definitely excitement.

Still, he said: 'Boss is it ok if I just take a day to decide? I just want to talk to Kutenda. I can't just – you know – '

'Of course. Someone from head office will probably phone you before the end of the week. They're obviously looking for an immediate start. Your flight and moving costs will be covered.'

Goodwin thought about the three kitbags he owned which would be ample for his worldly possessions. The company would score on the 'moving costs' front. But wow. A *flight* to Joburg. No mind-numbing, nausea-inducing eternity wedged inside a Translux bus.

'And boss – do you know if any of the other waiters – '

'Three Zimbos,' Adrian smiled. 'Staying together in a digs in Kempton Park. There's a room to rent. But no pressure. Again, I don't actually want you to go.'

Goodwin's shift that morning had been a blur. *Joburg. Joburg. Joburg.* New possibilities thrummed through his thoughts as he smiled, poured, delivered, smiled.

He'd spoken to Kutenda that night.

'Come with me, man. There'll be something for you there. Clean start. And maybe I can convince Aneni to come.' Goodwin's sister hovered constantly, darkly, in the recesses of his mind. The news about her, from their mom, was seldom good. The latest was she'd left Bulawayo on a bus to Blantyre. No goodbyes – though it seemed she was quite happy to keep receiving Goodwin's monthly EcoCash contributions.

Kutenda's face looked worse, having had twenty-four hours to swell with self-pity and indignation. His eyes held a soft, raw look – like his soul really had been exposed by the beating.

'Sho' brother. Why not?' he'd managed a tired smile. 'Could we share that room though?'

'We'll pay. They'll be good with extra rent, fo'sho.'

Goodwin offered up a silent prayer that the Zimbabwean waiters who were (allegedly) willing (should he take the job) to rent a room to their new manager, would be willing to take in Kutenda too.

He'd been doing it more and more. Quick silent prayers. Navigating pavements and taxis and orders and customers day in and day out – he'd found himself talking to God. It no longer felt farfetched at all to believe God was actually listening, and God actually cared.

It had started the night of the shooting. Something had snapped open inside of him as he wept over the girl's Bible, unleashing a longing he'd never known, and still didn't understand.

He'd kept the Bible under his bed with his clothes and the three kitbags and on and off over the past months he'd gone back to page – pause – read – pray. And somehow, a tender but tenacious faith had taken root.

Within a week of accepting the transfer offer, all the necessary strings had been pulled and Goodwin was surprised by the jolts of anticipation that would arrest him mid-task. He couldn't remember when last he'd so keenly felt the possibility of freedom. His co-workers had thrown him a farewell of sorts – leftover muffins and flatbreads after closing – overwhelming him with ten and twenty rand notes – hard-earned tips – pressed into his palms. He'd paid half of Kutenda's bus ticket to Johannesburg. 'Eish, sorry for you,' he'd laughed, slapping his friend on the back in mock sympathy. 'I'll wave from the sky.' The Trend head office had texted confirmation of Goodwin's Kulula flight and Kutenda had mocked back, 'What are you, a white guy now with your flight ticket?'

They'd gathered their courage and what was theirs to pack up in their Woodstock flat, and handed over the key to Frieda, who'd said, by way of an unemotional goodbye, *'Ja, weg is julle.'*

Adrian had offered to drive him to the airport, so Goodwin had made his swansong journey to Camps Bay – walk-taxi-walk. He somehow couldn't bring himself to go into the café for the last time. Famous was sitting on the pavement. Goodwin wandered over and sat down next to him, both men absentmindedly facing the sea, feet in the street.

The security guard sat on the pavement a lot more these days. Since the shooting, he'd lost something of his wild and warm gregariousness. He no longer *enthused* tourists into parking bays. Just waved and whistled.

'Eh I'll miss you, brother,' said Goodwin, as if to the sea.

'Ja and even me, I'll miss you. But maybe we'll be seeing each other, eh,' said Famous. He smiled a little. 'If there's good jobs there – Gauteng – you must WhatsApp.'

'Fo'sho. You're *famous* Famous!' joked Goodwin.

Famous laughed. 'Ah, no brother. Not famous enough.'

'You know what, hey?' Goodwin had a keen feeling this was a now-or-never convo. 'Being famous – being important – comes from doing important things. Things that are not about you. You're doing famous, important things every day. You did a famous, important thing – that day even. With the guns and that girl.'

A bus accelerated past, belching fumes. Waves crashed. The men sat.

Then suddenly –

'You read the white girl's Bible, hey?' Famous blurted. 'The other day, you were saying to Ivy when you walked here – about the Scriptures?'

'Sho', I've been reading a bit,' Goodwin said, a question in his voice.

'If God made the sea and the mountain and Jesus loves us like they say in the church – why didn't He stop the *tsotsis* shooting her?'

Goodwin hadn't expected this. Maybe the finality of knowing they'd probably never see each other again had made Famous bold to go there. More cars roared and braked in the road and Goodwin gathered his thoughts.

'I don't know, brother. I really don't know. I've asked also. But I know God *can* do those things – He *can* stop the *tsotsis*. And I know sometimes He waits, and it feels like He does nothing but He's never doing nothing, you know? And I think all the reading, it's making me see that – meanwhile – while I wait and while I don't understand all the things – I can trust Him.'

'Ok,' Famous said, 'Ok. I must maybe also find a Bible hey?' He smiled and then Adrian was there bleeping his car open and Goodwin was heaving his bags into the boot. Famous stood – shook his hand – and Goodwin knew this last minute of their friendship – their casual friendship based purely on workspace proximity – had been the most significant. Famous was woefully out of touch with his inner child and his shadow self and other things Goodwin had overheard white women talking about over their lattes at Trend. Yet his soul seemed nonetheless wide open to the work of God.

And now, here Goodwin was, in the teeming heart of Africa's biggest, busiest airport, and loving it.

He – and two days later, Kutenda – had settled quickly and uncomplicatedly into the commune of Zimbabwean waiters. When he came back to the house after a shift and someone cracked a joke in Shona and everyone *got it* – it felt like taking off a pair of shoes he'd been wearing for far too long, having only just figured they were also far too tight. He felt like he could breathe again. He felt free.

Still, he came into work earlier than necessary most days, profoundly at home, too, with the grind-shush-swish of coffee-making. As manager he wasn't, strictly speaking, supposed to be on barista duty, but was loath to lose touch with the process that kept customers coming. The mantle of managerial authority rested more comfortably on him than he thought it might, and he didn't feel the need to set himself loftily apart from his staff.

Everywhere he went, he took the Bible with him. He would read passages aloud to Kutenda at night – and then to his housemates – and that had morphed into a sort-of-official Bible study. He wasn't sure if the other waiters shuffled into the lounge and slouched on the seedy, Gumtree-bargain couches to listen because they wanted to, or because he was the boss. Either way, he was increasingly stirred to pour into them the truth of this Heavenly Father he was growing to know and love.

They were working their way through the gospel of Luke. Goodwin would read a few verses. Kutenda would nod and say with feeling things like, 'Yoh! That one. It's good.' Goodwin would agree – read a bit more – then close in prayer for their jobs, their safety, their families in Zim. And always he ended with something he'd heard at the church he visited on the odd off-weekend: 'Use us, however You choose, for Your glory.'

Next customer. *Ah!* A regular. The stunning flight attendant who ordered flat whites. His smile was genuine. Hers was polite.

'Good morning welcome to Trend what can I get you?'

Her face relaxed a little and she laughed. 'You mean you seriously don't know?'

Goodwin chuckled, 'Yes I do know. Sorry. Habit.'

He noticed how she held herself. The deep surreptitious breath in – the slow exhale – like she was trying to calm down but didn't want people to notice.

'Except, actually,' said Goodwin. 'Today I'm getting you an Americano with pouring cream.'

He never did this. What was he thinking? She was the customer and she wanted her flat white. But there was no one else waiting just then and he had time to chat and he felt a powerful urgency to see this woman – to really see her – and to act on the quickening that said she needed something different.

'What, *wena?*' another laugh – almost an undignified snort. Her tightly-wound words seemed suddenly un-sprung. 'No no. That's too much fat. The cream. Uh-uh. Next thing my skirt is too tight and I split the seams somewhere up there!' She rolled her eyes and gestured skyward where she'd soon find herself dutifully offering plastic cups of wine in muted tones up and down cramped aisles.

Goodwin laughed too. 'Trust me, this is what you need.' He went ahead and poured the coffee and the cream and his own boldness surprised him and he still didn't understand why he was doing this and he wasn't very practised at recognising God-moments but he knew this was one. God had something for this woman. Here and now. This moment.

She tapped her credit card. He scrawled her name and pushed the coffee smoothly across the counter.

'Where today?' he asked. 'Barcelona? New York?'

'Geneva.' She took a hot sip. And to her unreserved surprise, tears brimmed. Goodwin stared.

'Sorry. I'm so sorry Thandeka.' He never used her name, other than to write it on her cup every other day. 'Let me get you the flat white. I'm sorry. I just – that was stupid of me.'

'It's ok,' she laughed a bit again, deliberately pulling herself together. 'It's the cream. It reminds me of home. My *gogo* would put it in our tea and *pap* if she could get it cheap from the farmers sometimes. It was the biggest treat. Made me feel rich and like anything was possible.'

The now-or-never feeling in Goodwin's gut reached something of a crescendo and he suddenly had clarity. He said –

'It's true.'

'What's true?'

'You're rich and anything's possible.'

Thandeka shook her head – gave Goodwin a crazy-guy look – and took another sip. But whatever had been resting heavily on her shoulders seemed to lift a little. 'No. Not rich. And no, not everything is possible.'

Now Goodwin was on a roll – excited and enjoying himself and focused entirely on whatever weighed down this woman's soul and not at all focused on whether or not this encounter was awkward.

'Not rich with money and stuff, maybe,' he said. 'But you can be rich in love. God pours out His love for us – like cream, but more. And richer and thicker. And it never runs out and you get it for free.'

It was Thandeka's turn to stare.

'So anyway.' Goodwin felt suddenly self-conscious, but he was ok with it. 'I think God wants you to have cream today, and I think He wants you to know He loves you, and that He knows about your dreams and even if it seems impossible nothing gets in the way of His plans.'

Thandeka was silent for several sips.

'Thank you,' she said finally, fresh tears welling. 'Thank you. For ignoring my wishes for a flat white.' They both laughed. 'For the cream. For reminding me. It's just that – I don't know – it's hard to *feel* that love, you know? When it just feels like nothing I do is good enough. Like no matter how hard I try – ' Her voice gave way. She shrugged and she stared down at what was left of her coffee.

Suddenly the words Goodwin had read in the lounge the night before skipped across his thoughts. Luke six somewhere. Jesus was talking. Verse thirty-seven? Thirty-eight?

'Give, and you will receive. Your gift will return to you in full – pressed down, shaken together to make room for more, running over, and poured into your lap. The amount you give will determine the amount you get back.'

Slowly he reached below the counter to the shelf where he kept his stuff during shifts.

'Take this.'

He slid the Bible towards Thandeka.

'It was given to me – in a way,' he said. 'The underlining and stuff isn't all mine. Mostly it isn't mine. But it's helped me, you know? I think maybe – just read a bit. And ask Him.'

'I can't take your Bible, no,' Thandeka protested. But Goodwin saw in her eyes the hunger – the intrigue – the hope.

'Yes you can. I'm in charge today remember?' he joked, looking down and waving her away. 'No flat white for you. Cream. The Bible.'

She lifted the Bible gingerly – still unsure – 'What? *Really?*' – slipped it into her carryon – a red daypack that looked unlikely on her sophisticated person – and smiled.

'Well. This was the weirdest coffee of my life,' she said loudly and lightly – though she didn't seem to be forcing. 'Next time, flat white, you hear?'

April
2 0 1 6

'Everything you've ever wanted is on the other side of fear.'

George Addair

9

Durban

'Certainly, travel is more than the seeing of sights; it is a change that goes on, deep and permanent, in the ideas of living.'

Miriam Beard

'You cleaned up good.' Bryce was grinning as he came into their room, car keys jingling his readiness to get going. Jules was wearing a black shift dress and heels. She'd also put on her pearls even though she worried they made her look old, but he was admiring her with unveiled pleasure.

'Even you,' she said, laughter lurking just beneath a sultry smile. The kids were being fed and fussed over in the kitchen by a new-ish babysitter – a seventeen-year-old they knew from church who was probably too young and definitely too enthusiastic but adequately responsible to handle spaghetti bolognaise in her hair for one evening. Bryce had made reservations for them at 9th Avenue Waterside. This warm autumn night was about to belong completely to Bryce and Jules, and to them alone.

The reason for their date night was the big reveal of Bryce's big plan, which was supposed to be a surprise, and which he suspected was not. They had a No Secrets marital policy and though gifts, and surprise dinners or trips, didn't fall under the jurisdiction of said policy, fourteen years of honest marriage had made it almost impossible for Bryce to keep anything from her.

The inflight magazine had been next to her bed for the longest time. It was one of his many small missed-you presents, brought home to her after one of his many not-so-small client meetings. He was always buying her gifts or bringing her free stuff that made him think of her when he wasn't home. It was his love language. It wasn't her love language. They both knew it, but he couldn't help himself, and she graciously received it all like she was fluent in that dialect. He knew she was an *experience* person, not a *thing* person. He also knew he'd brought home dozens of other magazines, which she would read with mild interest and then surrender to Mia's purple Hello Kitty scissors or the recycling bin.

Clearly, this magazine was different. He'd caught her staring at the cover when she didn't know he was watching, and something in her look of longing – quickly replaced by resignation – had arrested him.

And so he decided one morning as they flossed side by side and he made mock-sexy eyes at her in their bathroom mirror and she simultaneously laughed and flossed, that he would take Jules to France. He would find those exact lavender fields. He would pray for just such a magazine-worthy sunset to alight on the place. He would make her happy.

In the quiet moments he found himself alone – waiting in an airport lounge, being shuttled to meetings – his thoughts about Jules turned sad. He replayed their conversation on the bed, last winter. He worried over her yearning for purpose and fulfilment. He felt guilty that she'd put her dreams on hold for him and the kids because, forget organs: she was a Life Donor. He felt guilty that he wasn't around much. The nuts and bolts of what constituted their lives fell almost entirely on her.

As they sped along Ruth First Highway over Blue Lagoon and it sank in that there were no kids in the car singing or giggling or swallowing things they shouldn't, Bryce felt like his soul might be catching up with his body and he exhaled as if he hadn't for days. At last they could talk like grownups on a date.

'I just hate all this traveling, babe,' he said, putting a hand on her leg and changing lanes. 'Can't I get a sponsor? A patron? Then I could be home for the kids' bath time and bedtime. I could stir whatever you've got going on the stove. As a sauce stirrer – even a cheese grater – I think I could be fairly quick out of the blocks!'

Jules laughed. 'Dude,' she said. 'You've just got to find a way to use guilt to your advantage. Like me.'

For several months, she'd been baking and selling her Lunchbox Luxuries. To dull the ache of self-reproach (because she couldn't clean up all the world's litter), she'd set up a website, intent on feeding the school children of Durban with healthy snacks.

'I'm rolling mom guilt the way some people roll debt, see?' she told Bryce in what he called her Business Plan Voice. 'These working moms are totally wracked with guilt. They need a guilt management approach. How better to assuage their lousy-parent culpability than with gluten-free, sugar-free, fun-free kid food? They can't be at the matches or the recitals. Oh no! They can't help with homework. Calamity! But at least their offspring are being bolstered by chia seeds, right? Because, #antioxidants. Also, #FirstWorldProblems.'

He laughed out loud because she was all about the hashtags. 'You should put that on your CV as part of your skill set,' he said. '"Adept at hashtaggery."' Earlier that day she'd surreptitiously texted him a photo of an elderly lady in Woolworths with disturbingly – alarmingly – violet hair and –

#PurpleRinseBrigade.

But for all their banter, he'd still been worried, and the worry had galvanized him into securing at least one of his wife's dreams, by planning and booking and organising a lavender-tinted experience of a lifetime. And tonight, at her favourite restaurant, he was going to surprise her (or not), and tell her.

'Right this way,' smiled a waiter as they stepped into the tranquillity and understated luxury that accompany fine dining everywhere in the world. They took their seats at a table overlooking the harbour. Wine glasses and sparkling water arrived.

'Ooh, we *are* going big tonight,' Jules joked, adding in her movie-trailer accent: 'Not just *ordinary* water. *Sparkling* water!' She squeezed Bryce's hand. Neither of them drank wine unless they absolutely had to, to be polite. Bryce could afford to buy her the best champagne on the menu, but he knew her better than that. There really was nothing she'd rather drink than water with bubbles.

'Shoo. This is beautiful,' she said seriously. Then – 'So when are you going to tell me?'

Bryce cracked up. 'No way! You're impossible. *How?* How did you know?'

'The magazine was missing from my bedside table for a couple days. Then it was back.' Jules was grinning like she'd won an enormous prize. 'Thank you, Bryce. Thank you thank you thank you.' Uncharacteristically, she teared up. She didn't want to come up with a clever chirp. She really was just unbelievably grateful.

'Ok so – ' Bryce relaxed. She knew. Now he could just enjoy unpacking the details. 'Unfortunately we can't go this year, because of my Dad's 70th thing in Plett. I really wanted to squeeze in both, but with the kids already – '

'Of course,' she nodded, still smiling.

'So this is crazy long in advance, to even be telling you and all, but then I figured you probably already knew – '

'Which I did, because #notjustaprettyface.'

'Exactly,' he laughed. 'So I hope you're ok to wait, but I so badly wanted to give you something to look forward to. And all this – this is not guilt management. This is just because I love you.' Bryce got a bit choked up at this point – which made Jules weepy again – which then made her laugh.

'Gosh, we're getting old. Our one night out, and we sit here crying.' She tried hard – almost successfully – to pull herself completely together, and said, 'You know, I feel like so much of my life has been just *getting through stuff*. Like, I'm *waiting* to live, until I can get to the *actually living* part. But really, it's all living, right? So this next year and a bit – until we go – I don't just want to get through it, to get to France. I want to live it. I want to enjoy it. With you.' She smiled. 'And then, we can go to France.'

'I like that idea very much, Mrs McIntosh,' said Bryce, his gaze not leaving hers.

That night, they ordered sumptuous plates of prawns and held hands and the sparkling water flowed like all the dreams they were dreaming and Bryce kept thinking about what Jules had said – how they should just enjoy this next year and whether it's school runs in Durban or lavender fields in France, it's all living.

He kept thinking how they had No Secrets but how she'd said it like she knew something he didn't.

10

Montreal

'Questions you cannot answer are usually far better for you than answers you cannot question.'

Yuval Noah Harari

The airline always booked them into one of three hotels, all within a five-kilometre radius of Montreal-Pierre Elliot Trudeau International Airport.

'This one's the nastiest,' Gillian growled to Thandeka as the shuttle deposited them with their neat, modest luggage at a nondescript hotel entrance at 6:15am after a sleepless flight. The two women had worked business class from Frankfurt, ferrying what seemed like endless drinks and snacks and socks and hot towels to the assortment of wealthy yet equally travel-dishevelled passengers.

'Definitely,' agreed Thandeka. 'But closest to the river,' she added with a smile. She loved the St Lawrence River, chunks of ice still afloat at this time of year. The first time she'd flown to Montreal in what the Canadians optimistically called 'spring', she'd hung on to the riverbank railings with gloved hands and laughed out loud at the frosted world before her.

She'd never admit this to Gillian – a white girl who came from money and had fierce opinions and impossibly high standards – but Thandeka didn't really care which hotel they slept in. If she translated *stiff white linen* and *free soap* into the language of her upbringing, it still spelled out something like *adventure*, and something like *miracle*. *Simangaliso*, she thought.

She had soon realised that – mostly – the world over – an airport's an airport's an airport. In dazed, exhausted moments, she sometimes had to remind herself where in the world she was, because too many terminals looked and smelt and felt identical. Duty-free outlets sold the same expensive perfume and booze. Food courts sold the same mass-produced, plastic-encased sandwiches, salads and unexceptional pastries.

Hotels – especially the big chains they so often slept in – also looked and smelt and felt identical. But Thandeka didn't mind. The cookie-cutter rooms she'd occupied – in Scotland, Austria, Greece and countless other countries – gave her a sense of normalcy and stability within the haphazard shift-scheduling and sleep deprivation her job exacted.

And for Thandeka, these layovers were all about taking to the streets. When the rest of the cabin crew would go drinking or shopping, she would divide her time between sleeping, and walking.

She never got tired of stepping out onto the sidewalks of cities around the globe and being swallowed by the fumes of foreign cars and languages. She would walk and walk and walk and imbibe every sight and smell until she absolutely had to sit down on a park bench or at a pavement café.

'I'm thinking a shower, then a martini,' Gillian sighed as they wheeled their bags into an elevator bound for the eighth floor. 'I'm shattered. You got the key?'

'Yip,' said Thandeka. '801.'

Predictably, theirs was the first twin room in the thickly carpeted corridor. They each laid claim to an enormous double bed. Dumped bags. Kicked off shoes. Thandeka set her phone alarm for five hours' time – then sunk body and soul into the crisp covers. Gillian headed straight for the shower, but not before chiding Thandeka –

'Seriously? You're not going to come for breakfast with us? *Again?*'

Thandeka knew Gillian would be meeting the rest of the crew in the hotel dining room within the hour for hot food and too-early alcohol and inevitable hook-ups that wouldn't happen if no one was tired or tipsy.

'Sleep summons. I must obey,' Thandeka said, not even opening her eyes.

'Girl, you have *got* to get a life,' Gillian reproached for the many-eth time. Yet every time she said it, it sounded less convincing. It came with less derision – more wistfulness. Thandeka wondered when her friend would get tired of the drinking and flirting and regret.

Thandeka remembered a time when she would've felt the sting of FOMO. Now, she just chuckled softly and half asleep from her pillow, so very glad to be where she found herself. Her laughter came easy these days. Less like a pent-up, stricken, burst of mirth. More like she was truly happy. Truly free.

'I'll get another key at reception,' said Gillian. 'Lock up if you go out.'

'Be good,' Thandeka mumbled.

Five hours and one deep sleep later, Thandeka exited the hotel, drawing joyous mouthfuls of fresh, freezing air and falling into a brisk rhythm that conveyed her in the direction of the river.

An hour after that, having filled her lungs with 'overseas air' – it still thrilled her – and feasted her eyes on the St Lawrence, she crossed the road, away from the river, and pushed open the glass doors of a Tim Hortons, because, *I'm in Canada*, she thought with delight. Warmth and coffee and grilled cheese greeted her.

'*Bonjour,*' she tried. '*Je voudrais* – um – just a coffee, please. And actually,' because she was suddenly aware she hadn't eaten since just before landing, 'also, a maple-dip donut?' She was still just a little too flight-weary for beginner French. Too happy – because again, *I'm in Canada!* – to choose anything other than a maple-syrup-something.

She headed to a booth with her North American indulgences – sighed into a red leather seat – and reached into her daypack for the barista's Bible.

She was hungry for it. Hungrier even than she was for the donut, which, she had to admit, never tasted as good as it looked. 'Feed an appetite and it grows,' *gogo* used to say with dangerously raised eyebrows. The context of her caution was usually sex, but Thandeka had lived long enough to know it was true of most things. For sure, it was true of this Bible – this weird gift she'd received nine months ago from a near stranger. The more she read, the more she wanted to read. Her appetite for truth was growing – and she was feeding it – and still it grew.

Thandeka fed the appetite in rare moments alone, strapped into a bulkhead seat when the cabin lights were dimmed and most passengers slept or binge-watched movies on their tiny screens. She would skim gospel pages or read a psalm. Lately, she'd been gripped by the stories of Jesus – everything He said, everything He did. He was all about the poor, the downtrodden, the marginalised. It seemed the only people He criticised were the stiff, religious, box-ticking Pharisees and others like them.

Others like gogo, she couldn't help thinking.

This Jesus who showed Himself to be so gentle, so compassionate – she wanted to know Him. She began to imagine (*It can't be possible*, she would think, *or can it?*) that this Jesus loved her, even if her skirt were too short. And yet, more and more, she wanted Him to choose the length of her skirt. She wanted Him to think her skirt was just right.

Time turned her coffee lukewarm. Her donut was pocked with perfunctory, disinterested nibbles. Utterly absorbed, she devoured the gospels – skipped Acts – paged on to Romans.

Then she felt the fizz. The gut-simmer.

She'd never talked about it to anyone because, who was there to tell? (She pictured wandering into the cockpit somewhere over the Atlantic:

'So, Craig, has the Holy Spirit ever spoken to you?' Maybe *not*.) Also, she couldn't be *absolutely* sure. Yet she was *almost wholly* convinced it was God. She wouldn't have known how to describe it to someone, other than that it felt like a Cal-C-Vita was effervescing in her soul. She knew He was guiding her through the pages. She knew He wanted to show her something.

A waiter startled her –

'*Tout est bon?*'

Thandeka had no idea what he'd said but he was giving her a cheerful thumbs up, so she nodded and gave him an absentminded smile. She looked back down to the Bible – her eyes catching the hotel keyring poking from her red, unzipped daypack.

801.

The Bible was open at Romans chapter eight. Much of it was highlighted or underlined, by the barista or whoever had held this Bible before him.

801? She asked herself, and no one, and maybe God. Could she even *ask* Him random stuff like that? How involved was He *really* in the detail?

Yes, 801, came a soft, strong thought.

The Cal-C-Vita was seriously fizzing now. She read. Romans eight. Verse one.

'*So now there is no condemnation for those who belong to Christ Jesus.*'

'Excuse me, do you have the time perhaps?' Startled again – by the verse, by the voice – Thandeka looked up into the face of an elderly woman – clearly British from her accent, clearly a tourist from her array of luggage.

'Um – ' Thandeka grabbed her phone and actually yelped. 'No! Sorry – yes. It's half past four.' She hurriedly scooped her things back into her daypack – abandoned the donut and coffee – burst out into the shock of late afternoon chill and ran into the street. She ran all the many blocks back to the hotel – her shins sending stabbing warnings to her brain that she was not, in fact, wearing running shoes.

Her crew was due back at the airport at 6pm. She got back to the hotel just after five. Tearing through the lobby and into an elevator she gasped for breath. It was then she realised she was smiling, despite the stress of running – and running late.

'Thandeka! What the hell?' Gillian looked up from zipping closed her cases, already dressed to kill – or at least, dressed to serve chicken or beef.

'Lost track of time,' Thandeka panted, grinning. She walked straight into the bathroom, blasted open the shower taps and within about eleven minutes, if anyone was counting, she had showered, changed into a fresh uniform, and crammed shut her bags.

Gillian just stared.

'I'll do my makeup in the shuttle,' said Thandeka, still grinning, and still slightly out of breath. 'It'll be ok. Sorry I made you stress.' Despite Gillian's consternation and palpable iciness, Thandeka hugged her.

Then she slung the daypack over her shoulder and wheeled her case towards the elevator, Gillian in hurried pursuit.

As their shuttle careened through traffic and Thandeka willed her mascara brush to stay steady, she was nonetheless light with expectation and revelation –

Because there's no condemnation, no condemnation, no condemnation, for those who belong to Christ Jesus.

The truth rolled around her thoughts like a bright thing she wanted to touch and smell and hold up to her cheeks. The barista had told her, that day at O.R. Tambo, she was rich and anything was possible. She got it. It was this thing of being utterly un-condemned. Rich in love. Rich in grace.

And maybe God really did have some sort of anything's-possible plan for her life.

11

Montreal

'I haven't been everywhere, but it's on my list.'

Susan Sontag

Despite his privileged, private-school past and all the traveling he'd done, Drew had never had a white Christmas. Which is why he'd left Istanbul in September of the previous year, on a flight to Toronto.

They *should* have had a white Christmas the year Drew turned ten. The year of the yelling and the crying. The year his dad left them. The trip, and life as he understood it, was cancelled.

So really, you do still owe me this.

He mentally – flippantly – flicked the sentiment in the direction of Australia as he tapped his dad's credit card number into his phone to book yet another ticket to yet another place on the planet that caught his fancy.

He reckoned he'd pull into Canada in time to see the autumn leaves everyone raved about and he'd try to remember to call it *fall* and he'd keep up his English teaching when he wasn't seeing the sights and meeting the girls.

Then he'd figure out something epic for Christmas.

He'd once shared a room with a Canadian, in a youth hostel in Bangkok. The guy's name was *Tyler* – Tyler Tremblay – and they were in

Thailand, and as corny as it seemed on reflection, at the time the name-rhyming-joke and a bit of boozing was enough upon which to build a shallow friendship that now mostly consisted of them following each other on Instagram where Drew's presence was at best sporadic. Drew DM'd Tyler –

Bro! It's been too long!

And after some back and forth, Tyler seemed pretty sure he could organise a job for Drew at Searchmont, a ski resort near Lake Superior and Ty's hometown of Sault Ste Marie, Ontario.

The following months rolled out just as Drew had pictured them, which took him a little by surprise. He liked to imagine people saw him as a roll-with-the-punches, rugged adventurer, good-looking even when he hadn't showered for days, and unfazed by the detours, delays and inevitable disappointments of life lived everywhere and out of a backpack. But in honest moments, Drew admitted to himself he was no longer totally up for the downs of travel. Now and then, he just wanted predictability, and a plan.

Canada offered him both.

He had a steady stream of English students. He would wake up at 5am Toronto time to give lessons to South Koreans hurrying home from work to find Drew waiting for them on their screens with a rigorous exposé of apostrophes of possession and contraction. Then he would lose himself in an ellipsis of museums and coffee shops, his days further punctuated by tram trips to laundromats and 7-Elevens.

From Toronto he flew to Vancouver, then took a train to Banff National Park where he was quietly spellbound by the red and gold iridescence of the trees. He saw the sights. He met the girls. (Although, with a sage sobriety that made him feel like a proper grownup, he avoided the no-strings-attached hook-ups he'd habitually enjoyed in the past, because he'd been traveling long enough to know there were *always* strings attached.)

In late October he headed back to Ontario. Courtesy of Ty's brother-in-law he'd landed the promised ski resort job, board and lodging part of the package. Surrounded by people – indisputably nice, plaid-clad people – Drew settled into the routine of work and rest and community. He mostly managed the ski equipment hired out to the plethora of tourists and eager beginners. It wasn't the most stimulating work he'd ever done, but he liked it, and he liked the *poutine* in the cafeteria and the silence of the slopes after dark.

More than that, he liked spending weekends with Tyler and his family in Sault Ste Marie. He got no special-guest treatment. It was like he was genuinely a son in the house. It was an unspoken expectation that he would do dishes and laundry and get texted to pick up milk from Pino's on his way over. And it was a given that he would be invited and included into every familial moment of these people who laughed hard and often, gave generously and with unreserved delight, loved deeply and freely. It was also a given that he would tag along with them to church if he happened to wake up under their roof on a Sunday, and because he was with the Tremblays, church wasn't as awful as he'd feared.

'You're different to what I remember from Bangkok,' he'd said to Ty one Saturday morning in mid-December as they fried eggs on his mom's grimy, homely stove and flurries of snow laced the windowpanes.

Ty chuckled. 'Yeah. I wasn't in a great space, eh? In Bangkok. Too much beer. Too much of the old electric spinach!'

Drew felt the inner cringe of condemnation. He wasn't exactly seeking out drugs like he had during one crazy semester at varsity. (And that month in Réunion.) But he still rolled a joint when he got the chance.

He was intrigued, nonetheless. 'So what's changed?' he asked.

'You really wanna know?' Ty was smiling down into the sizzling pan, spatula playing at the eggs' crisping edges.

'Sure.'

'Um. Dude. Don't think I'm weird or anything. But it's Jesus, you know?

85

Like, I just got to a point where I knew my life was falling apart. I had no direction, no purpose. I was spiralling. Hurting people, hurting me. And I guess I just cried out to God in the freefall and He caught me.'

Ty flipped two eggs onto a plate. Drew said nothing. Ty went on in his Canadian lilt, over-easy like the eggs –

'I always knew the truth, growing up. I mean, you've seen my parents. They're freakin' saints.' (Drew *had* seen Ty's parents and they *were* freakin' saints. He still wasn't used to how kind they were to each other.) 'But it was never real to me. I'd never owned it. Then suddenly God had my attention and I was, like, *right*... Actually I'm screwed and Jesus is my only hope out of the screw-up.'

Drew shifted uncomfortably on his chair. It was one thing to deny the existence of God – to take an abstract, philosophical stance. It was quite another to deny the existence of a transformed human wearing sweatpants and frying Saturday morning eggs.

'Dude, your eggs are getting cold,' Ty laughed.

'Oh. Ja.' Drew's accent was always strongest in pensive, unguarded moments. 'But like, anyone can change, right? So you made some new choices. Broke some bad habits. That's not to say the whole Jesus vibe is for real.'

'Yeah that's what I used to think. But I realised I *couldn't* break those habits on my own. Maybe there are stronger people than me, with stronger willpower? But even if I could have changed my behaviour, only God could have changed my heart. Like, for real.'

'Huh,' said Drew matter-of-factly, the way a tolerant, you-do-you Gen-Z should. Then, because the convo was getting too serious, and because his pride compelled him to make it clear he wasn't relinquishing his doubts or disparagement, he added, 'These eggs are f***ing amazing.'

A week later, Drew got the white Christmas of his ten-year-old dreams. There was gift-opening in pyjamas, an appropriately cheerful iTunes

86

Christmas carol playlist, hot chocolate, and over-the-top lights in every window on the street. The Tremblays drove him to Harmony Beach on Lake Superior where waves lapped at the snow and Drew learned that Ty's sisters could throw snowballs harder than anyone and then back at the house there was a turkey the size of a small child and so much dessert and Drew forgot to be cool and cynical.

They'd also gone to church on Christmas Eve. And lying at last on the lounge sleeper couch more than twenty-four hours later – happy, stuffed, and a little peopled-out – phrase fragments drifted in and out of Drew's mind – the words the pastor had read from some prophet book – Zephaniah?

For the LORD your God is living among you.

He is a mighty saviour.

He will take delight in you with gladness.

With His love, He will calm all your fears.

He will rejoice over you with joyful songs.

Drew shoved a pillow over his head in a futile attempt to drown out what was coming from within. Eventually, he slept.

Two months later, he left Searchmont, Sault Ste Marie and the Tremblays to see more of Canada. He checked into a yurt in Algonquin National Park, hooked up to the Wi-Fi of the park's Welcome Centre, taught English, read thirteen books, and marvelled at ambling moose and badger dams and his growing loneliness.

He spent March in Quebec City, and when April rolled around with the beginnings of a thaw, Montreal felt like the next good idea.

A fifty-minute flight landed him in the city of spires in the early evening, another francophone slice of Europe in the New World. Because he didn't really care where he stayed, he decided he'd get onto the first hotel transfer service he came across. He'd done exactly that, his attention briefly riveted as he waited on the curb to trade places with a uniformed crew of flight attendants alighting from the shuttle and hustling past him to get to a flight.

And so, here he was.

'*Votre clé, monsieur*,' the receptionist said. 'Enjoy your stay.'

'*Merci*,' Drew replied, scooping up the key and the credit card with one hand and without looking up. He wasn't in the mood for pleasantries. He was in the mood for escape which is what he planned to do the moment he got up to his room on the – *Which floor?* – he glanced at the keyring – *Eighth*.

Once he was out the elevator and through the door, he heaved his backpack onto the crisp white bedspread, unzipped a side pouch and fished around for a specific pair of black socks buried within. He unfurled them and dug inside one of the socks for a small Ziploc bag of *dagga*. It was the last of his stash from Istanbul. He hadn't smoked around the Tremblays. He'd hardly even smoked after hours at Searchmont. But tonight, he needed to throw off the horrid, heavy truth that he was no longer having a good time, and he no longer had any idea what came next.

He kicked off his boots. Leaned back on the plush headboard. Carefully tapped the marijuana onto a torn-off strip of the hotel writing pad. But reaching for his lighter on the bedside table he dropped the joint.

He swore loudly into the silent room with its no-smoking sign, rolled off the bed and crouched to feel for the small stick of escape he desperately wanted to light.

His fingers found metal. *Nail clippers? Gross.* And smooth leather.

He stared into the underbed gloom that a hurriedly shoved hotel vacuum cleaner had clearly missed. He pulled out a book with a brown, faux leather cover.

A Bible?

It wasn't a standard-issue Gideon's New Testament that might've been unsurprising in a room like this. The Bible, like the nail clippers, was a left-behind thing by someone who had packed quickly, distractedly.

Drew felt suddenly weird and hot and breathless. He got back onto the bed, his joint forgotten. Holding the Bible, he knew it must have been held a lot by somebody else. He knew without opening it that this somebody else had loved on the pages.

Anger and intrigue, fear and hope, doubt and years of disappointment, surged and ebbed on the currents of his mind. He thought he might puke.

He opened it.

The pages flopped and settled, thin but sure.

It was then that Drew stopped breathing altogether.

Zephaniah three. Verse seventeen.

The words were neatly highlighted in blue and it looked like whoever had done the highlighting had used a ruler so it occurred to him that this Bible must've belonged to a girl and he didn't read the words so much as they read him and he couldn't believe it – wanted to believe it – knew he shouldn't believe it. And yet – what if – *what if?* – what if it was true that –

'*…the LORD your God is living among you. He is a mighty saviour. He will take delight in you with gladness. With His love, He will calm all your fears. He will rejoice over you with joyful songs.*'

12

Johannesburg

*'That which we need the most will be found
where we least want to look.'*

Carl Jung

Drew would look back on the last days of April 2016 as a tornado of travel –
body and soul.

He wasn't sure how long he sat on that hotel bed in Montreal –
the open Bible on his lap, the open sluice gates of his soul flooding his
consciousness and spilling over onto his cheeks, the pillows, the pages. It
seemed heaven itself had opened above him and over him and he sensed a
presence he hardly dared to believe was real.

The ping and vibration of a text in his jeans pocket eventually
prompted him to let out an exhausted, almost euphoric breath, and pull out
his phone.

A three-minute voice note from his mom. It would be lunchtime in
South Africa.

Hello my boy! Mom here, came the first voice he'd loved, needlessly
introducing herself. (Why did old people do that?)

I hope you're safe and happy. Um, I think you're still in Canada hey?

Listen boy, you know there's no pressure from me – I know you're still enjoying romping around the world and all that. I just really felt – ag, I know you think I'm crazy – but I was praying for you – because like it or not I still do that – and I really felt I should tell you about an opportunity. Again, no pressure. Just put it in your pipe and smoke it, as they say. Though I do hope you're not doing too much of that, my love, it's so bad for your brain.

Anyway – sorry – so, um, last week at our ladies' Bible study, Leighann from our Missions Board told us about some folks who've planted a church near Monkey Bay, in Malawi. They've been meeting under trees and squashing into homes in the village when it rains, but the church is really growing and now some funding has come through from a non-profit type-thing in the States, I think, and anyway they want to build now, and they need an architect.

I know anything to do with church irritates you, boy, but I just thought maybe you'd enjoy using your degree a bit, in a way, and I don't think Malawi has been ticked off your list yet? Again, just a thought. Of course, if you flew into Joburg and then up to Blantyre, maybe you could stay a night? I'll cook whatever you like. Love you my darling. Missing you. Bye now.

What comes next? he'd wondered.

Well, this.

Drew smiled. And spluttered a bit through another bout of tears and he was glad he hadn't unpacked much more than his *dagga* socks because he pulled his boots back on and shoved the Bible into his backpack, briefly wondering, *Is this theft? Nah.* Then he went to the loo which wouldn't have happened in the movie of his life, but this was his *real* life and in this moment

– zipping his jeans – grabbing his stuff – then going back into the bathroom to flush the *dagga* because he was tired of hoping he wouldn't get caught by airport security – his real life had never before felt so real.

In the elevator back down to the lobby he sent his mom a shaky voice note in reply –

Howzit mom. Um – hi – thanks for your message. It's actually – shoo. I've got a lot to tell you. But um, I'm leaving for the airport now. I'm sure there'll be a flight to Joburg in the next ten hours or so. I'll definitely come home. Then, um, ja. Will you tell those mission people I'll go and help? Maybe just try get me details of who, how and where to, from Blantyre? I'll be in touch about my flights. Thanks so much Mom. Look forward to seeing you.

Then –

Love you.

Which he almost never said.

'There is a problem with the room, *Monsieur?*' asked the nonplussed receptionist when Drew dropped the key on her counter and announced he was checking out of the room he'd paid for hardly an hour before. He hadn't even taken anyone *with* him to the room, for that hour.

Drew looked at her this time, and smiled.

'No. No problem. Nothing wrong at all. It was the right room.'

There was no airport shuttle waiting so he ordered an Uber. Five minutes later he was in an old but carefully valeted Toyota with an overpowering air freshener dangling from the rear-view mirror and a driver who spoke to his GPS but not to Drew. He was on his way back to Montreal-Pierre Elliot Trudeau International Airport.

Hey Ty, he texted from the backseat, **flying home, then to Malawi to build a church, ha ha. U been praying or what?**

At the airport Drew went straight to the British Airways helpdesk because his dad preferred him at least to rack up frequent flyer miles, on Qantas or BA. Normally, Drew wouldn't bother. In fact, several times over the past couple of years, he had used any other airline simply *because* it offered a *more* expensive flight and would in no way benefit his dad. He noted the shift in his conscience.

Flip, Jesus, he thought. *Really? You're starting already?*

Economy was full. There were a few business class seats left on a flight leaving just before midnight. He cringed at the price. *Ah well. More miles for dad. And a proper sleep.*

He did the time-zone Math. There'd be a three-hour layover in London. He'd land in Johannesburg at 5am almost a calendar day and a half later, but in real-time just less than twenty-four hours from now. He texted his mom the flight details, and smiled as he re-read the flurry of surprised, cautiously excited but definitely concerned texts she'd sent since his voice note. Was he ok? Had something happened? What did he want her to make for dinner? He told her he could Uber from O.R. Tambo once he landed but he knew she'd be waiting at the arrivals barricade of Terminal A, with unmasked elation.

His backpack was weighed and tagged. He watched it disappear on the conveyer belt, knowing it would imminently be stowed in the bowels of the plane. The Bible was inside. He didn't want to read it on the plane the way he'd sometimes seen people doing. In fact, he didn't want to open it again. Not yet. He wasn't sure he was ready for more lashings of unconditional acceptance. It was all still too strange. Too surreal.

Yet the thrilling, bracing, bewildering winds of change continued to blow through his soul and his circumstances. In a matter of hours there had been a seismic shift in his worldview, and he had the freaked-out feeling this was only the beginning.

He whiled away the time in the departure lounge – on the flight – at Heathrow – on another flight – intermittently sleeping and allowing his windswept thoughts to swirl and settle into something of a way forward.

When it came to prayer, Drew had no idea what he was doing. But back on South African soil and waiting at a baggage collection carousel to be re-united with his backpack, he hoped-very-badly-in-the-direction-of-God that the Bible was still inside, even though he was too scared to read it again. He finally caught sight of his bag and hoisted it off the conveyor belt and suddenly all he could think was, *God, I hope very badly Mom really is here.*

She was. With all the tears and wild waving of a mother who hasn't hugged her son for the longest time. She had tried to be a warrior, but mostly she was a worrier, and her relief at seeing Drew was palpable. Drew's sister, Stella, and her husband, Mark, had come too. Drew and Stella had never been especially close, and Drew had been crap at keeping in touch with anyone at all, but he absolutely couldn't wipe the smile off his face at seeing them all there and he whooped, and hugged, and hugged everyone again.

Drew had landed on Wednesday, April 27th. It was a public holiday in South Africa. Freedom Day. The significance wasn't lost on him as he spent a day on his mom's shaded *stoep* in Houghton, talking and eating and laughing, then eating some more, intermittently taking sips of his childhood and swallowing down the previously un-savoured flavours of his newfound freedom.

He knew at some point he would have to explain things to his mom, who was circling carefully around the topic of why he would suddenly and immediately fly back to Africa to join a project that supported a cause he vehemently, mockingly opposed.

Mark and Stella stayed late into the afternoon. When they left after last hugs and promises to be less crap at keeping in touch, Drew followed his mom into the kitchen where she was about to start preparing more food.

'Mom,' he teased, perching on a barstool and leaning heavily on the counter, 'chill with the force feeding. They do have food in the northern hemisphere.'

'Ah! But do they have *bobotie*?'

'Fair enough,' Drew grinned. 'Keep going.' He paused, then –

'Mom can I tell you some stuff?'

She looked at him with wide eyes already brimming and he was suddenly freaked out again because he knew she'd been praying for this moment the better part of her life and he didn't want her gushing because he wasn't sure he could stand the emotional overwhelm.

'Ag no Mom!' he chided her with a laugh which cracked and collapsed into a sob and then she was embracing him and he was burying his face in her shoulder and haltingly it all came out.

He wept out the years of paralysing fear because maybe if he'd been better at cricket or soccer or anything at all, then his dad wouldn't have left. He wept out the excruciating pain of being rejected. Of watching his mom being rejected. And then the shame of imposing that rejection on so many people he loved – cold-shouldering anyone who could hurt him.

He told his mom about the drugs, the women, the selfish bastard he'd gotten comfortable being. The constant running away from anyone and anything that might hold a mirror to his life.

And then he told her about Canada – and the Tremblays – and the Christmas Eve service – and the hotel – and the Bible.

'It's like I've been running into the darkness this whole time – because I can just keep hiding there and doing my thing, you know?' he said, blowing actual snot bubbles. His mom pressed a tissue into his shaking hands. 'And then it's like, God flicked a switch and now everything's lit up and I can't run and hide in the dark anymore, and actually I don't want to.'

His mom's tears were streaming too, but she was calm. Smiling, nodding, not gushing. Drew went on.

'There's so much I don't get. There's so much – ' His voice broke off again.

'It's ok, my love. It's ok to have questions. I've still got questions, and I've known Jesus for decades. I think it's a pretty dangerous place to be if you *don't* have questions. But He'll begin to answer the questions, you'll see. Some of them at least. In time. And you'll learn to live with the tension of things left unanswered.'

Drew nodded and wiped his cheeks on his sleeves. 'It's just – I've been angry for so long and I'm not sure I really know what to do with that now, you know?'

His mom laughed. 'Go build a church.'

June
2 0 1 7

'I've been reading books of old
The legends and the myths
Achilles and his gold
Hercules and his gifts
Spiderman's control
And Batman with his fists
And clearly I don't see myself upon that list

But she said, where'd you wanna go?
How much you wanna risk?
I'm not looking for somebody
With some superhuman gifts
Some superhero
Some fairy tale bliss
Just something I can turn to
Somebody I can kiss

I want something just like this…'

Coldplay and the Chainsmokers

13

Monkey Bay

'Do all you can with what you have, in the time you have,
in the place you are.'

Nkosi Johnson

Goodwin was still nervous. He hadn't *seen* one of Lake Malawi's titanic crocodiles – but he'd heard the stories. And while the local kids splashed raucously in the shallows all day, their three-legged dogs stayed well away, eyeing the water with what must surely have been a cynicism and suspicion born of experience.

And so, Goodwin sprawled on the sand well away from the lake's lapping edges, watching the approach of the *Ilala*, Malawi's oldest passenger ferry, and breathing in the sounds of the market and the sun's sublime caress. It was June, and twenty-six degrees Celsius. This was about the coldest it got, his sister told him.

Aneni was the reason he was on a beach in Malawi. Over the years, his concern for her had mutated into full-blown fear – fuelled by frequent, frantic phone calls from their mother. The fragments of information that filtered through to the family – seldom from Aneni herself – suggested she was working as a prostitute somewhere near Lake Malawi. And despite the crackle and delay of their stilted, transborder phone calls, Goodwin had heard the shattering of his mother's heart.

It hadn't been a hard decision. He'd requested all his annual leave from the Trend directors and boarded a bus to find Aneni. Praying like he never had before, he traced every digital breadcrumb he could – scoured the Facebook pages of mutual Zimbabwean friends, watched for moments when she was online on WhatsApp. He knew she probably would've cut all contact if she didn't still need his money – which is eventually how he found her.

Aneni, I'm in Malawi. I've got cash for you. G.

He watched the two grey ticks. They turned blue. He waited.

Typing…

Then nothing. Then *Typing…* again.

Ok.

And a location pin.

Goodwin wondered – during the nerve-jangling, spine-rattling bus trip that took him from Blantyre to Monkey Bay where Aneni said she'd be waiting – whether she'd be brazen and cavalier, or shamefaced and apologetic.

She was neither. He saw her straightaway as he clambered down the bus steps, glad to have warm dust beneath his feet after hours of lurching and swaying. She smiled and he saw the girl in the woman and he smiled back and she was in his arms, holding on like she was afraid he might dissolve. *Thank God, thank God I came,* he thought.

'I've booked into a youth hostel. Got a double room,' he said when she'd finally let go of him and he'd retrieved his bag from the trailer which miraculously still clung to the back of the bus. He didn't want to ask where she was staying. He didn't want to see. He didn't want to know about pimps and clientele.

'Thank you,' she said softly.

'Well, you haven't seen it yet,' he laughed. 'It could be filthy.' Oh gosh. He was saying all the wrong things. *How filthy are the beds she sleeps in?*

'I just mean – thank you for coming.' It was Aneni's turn to feel awkward. A stretched bra strap kept slipping off her shoulder and she would hike it back up and under a grubby t-shirt with the words *Breathe Eezy* splashed across in glittered pink but minus most of the glitter. 'I know you're busy – with your big Joburg job.' She looked away, donning now what he could tell was a well-worn cloak of shame. There seemed nothing easy about the way she breathed – ensnared as she was to trade at a nightly market where she was the merch.

Goodwin stopped. And his tone stopped her: 'Aneni.' It was his older brother, no-nonsense voice. 'I came because I love you. We all love you. And yes, I have a big Joburg job. But you know what?' He smiled – relaxed a little. 'I'm not the main character of my story anymore. So, I'm free, I guess. Free to come chasing after my little sister.'

'Ok,' said Aneni quietly, a smile stealing back into her fretful eyes.

They spent the next few days like wary planets orbiting the obvious – unwilling to face its glare. But that left time enough to warm up to each other once again and they chatted like siblings should and like they always had as kids. She showed him around Monkey Bay. He was captivated by the vastness of the lake. He caught her up on news from family in Zim, and old school friends, cousins and acquaintances he'd met up with in Cape Town and Joburg.

And eventually – as gently as he could – one late afternoon on the same beach where he now sat, he grabbed hold of the tusks of the elephant that stood permanently between them in whatever hostel room or heaving market they found themselves.

Looking out at the lake he said, 'Aneni. This life – this – it's not God's best for you. You know that, sister. What happened? Why won't you come home? I don't want to make you feel guilty but you're killing our mother.'

He hadn't meant for his torrent of anguish to gush out quite like that, but, well, the elephant was lying down now – exhausted – and seemed to be saying, '*At last. Let's talk.*'

And so they did. Out came Aneni's fears and failures and her desperate need to feel loved by men because their own father had left so very long ago and Goodwin cried for how he could have, should have, loved her better.

'It wasn't you,' she kept saying. 'I just didn't know what to do. I wanted to climb outside of my skin – get away from myself somehow – and I guess I looked in the wrong places. Met the wrong people. And I know you've found God and all, but I can't see Him anywhere.'

Goodwin was quiet for a while. 'But sister, you know what your name means, don't you? Aneni. *God is with me.* He's been here all along. Been with you. Been with me. Been with mama even. And I know it's tough. Even me, I keep finding I must forgive our father again. Over and over. But also, we've got another Father, Aneni.'

She still wasn't buying anything from this Jesus guy, she told Goodwin. And he laughed and shook his head. 'You don't have to buy anything. He's got the bill. This one's on Him. He's paid it all.' Aneni looked at him like he really was *so* strange. So naïve. And he laughed harder.

'It's ok sister. There's no rush. God's got your number.'

'Oh my gosh. He's got the bill. He's got my number. He speaks in clichés and you are crazy, that's what I know.' But she couldn't keep from smiling at him.

'So since you're not buying any ideas from Jesus this afternoon, I'm wondering if you'll buy one from me.'

'Probably not,' she said, eyebrows raised, 'but you can try.'

'Come to South Africa with me. I want to start a business and I need your help. I've been saving and I'm nearly there – enough for a deposit anyway. I'm going to buy a franchise from Trend. Just a coffee truck – not a shop. And sell coffees and fancy hot drinks at markets and office blocks and – I don't know. I think it'll work.'

'You're going to buy a – ' Aneni shook her head, still smiling. 'Well. Ok.'

'Ok I'm definitely crazy? Or ok you'll come with me?'

'Both.'

That was almost a week ago. They were leaving Monkey Bay the next day.

The life Aneni had created for herself in her months in Malawi was meagre and desultory. Still, it hadn't been easy for her to disentangle herself from the demands and the sickening depravity of her bread-and-butter. Even now, as Goodwin watched the *Ilala* dock, Aneni was packing up the last of her Monkey Bay life by greeting friends. Women she'd worked with and wept with. Women whose hands she'd held as they'd visited so-called clinics for so-called safe abortions. Women she would truly miss, and if ever she did feel inclined to pray to Goodwin's God, she knew she'd be praying for them.

Goodwin watched the passengers alight from the ferry. Tourists – the white people. Locals – the black people.

And that guy. I can't tell, thought Goodwin. A white guy – mid, maybe late twenties. He had the at-home gait of a local – not at all out of place. Yet, the expensively stuffed backpack of a tourist.

The man reached into his jeans pocket for a ringing phone as he stepped down from the pier and onto the beach, heading in Goodwin's direction.

'Howzit, ma,' he said, and Goodwin smiled at the familiar accent. This guy sounded like so many of his Joburg customers and he was briefly homesick for the place that wasn't, strictly speaking, home. The man had slowed down to talk – absentmindedly kicking at sand – 'Ja, the bus leaves here at six tomorrow morning… That's right, flying from Blantyre tomorrow night… Thanks Mom… Thanks… Yes I'll send a screenshot now now…

Ok love you bye.'

The man loomed large before Goodwin and slipped his phone back into a pocket then –

'Dude! I'm so sorry man! I totally didn't see you!' He'd been looking down at the sand all the time and had ended the call inches from Goodwin – who had been unsure if he should speedily stand up and move out the way.

Instead, looking up, he laughed. 'No worries.' He couldn't help liking this open-faced young man who told his mom he loved her when she called. 'Forgive me for eavesdropping – I couldn't help overhearing your call – '

'Because I was about to stand on you.'

'Indeed,' nodded Goodwin. They both laughed. 'You said you're catching a bus to Blantyre tomorrow at six? So I think I'm on that same bus, but it's leaving at five-thirty.'

'Oh flip, hectic! Thanks bru! What are the chances – I nearly step on you and you save me from totally missing a bus – and a plane. Sorry man, I'm Drew.' Drew held out his hand to Goodwin and simultaneously sunk down next to him on the sand – 'Do you mind?' – dumping his backpack between them – 'This thing weighs a ton.'

'Goodwin.'

'Ah. From Zim,' Drew grinned. 'You guys have the best names on the continent.'

'And you're from South Africa,' Goodwin smiled knowingly, '*bru.*'

Immediately, they were friends, as happens when travel and the twists and turns of circumstance thrust people into unaffected conversation and they come to the unspoken agreement to forgo the customary relationship-building scaffolding of small talk. Drew's leading question – 'What brings you to Malawi?' – elicited a brief, honest account of Aneni's troubles and Goodwin's rescue operation and the goodness of God to answer prayer. Goodwin knew instinctively, by Drew's kind, unshielded manner, that he could speak freely.

'And you?'

Drew breathed out a laugh. 'Ha. You talk about the goodness of God, hey? That's, like, still quite a new concept for me. But I guess it's what brought me to Malawi.'

Goodwin was a comfortable, gentle listener – which turned Drew into an easy talker. It was as if Drew's story *wanted* to fall on Goodwin's ears. Drew told him about his family, his studies, his travels. He told him about his doubts, injuries and offences. He told him how he'd randomly found a Bible – 'I kept it; it's somewhere in here,' he said, giving his backpack an affectionate shove – and how God had used it to convince him that Jesus was for real.

He told Goodwin about the wondrous, uncanny timing of his mom's text and how he'd left Montreal and he'd seen a flight attendant at the airport that night and for some reason he would think about her at times the way he never thought about all the women he'd slept with and how he wanted to be able to look at a woman like that and know he could love her forever.

He told Goodwin about the months he'd spent helping some missionaries, and how he never thought he'd use his architecture degree and yet he had thrilled at the chance to design and advise and then see something he'd conceptualized turn tangible. He told Goodwin how good it felt to *help* – how it was the only thing that wrenched him out of his own head – and how his mom had been right all those years ago, saying the best way out of hopelessness is just putting your head down and using your gifts.

It was almost dark by the time Drew finished talking.

'Again, dude, I'm sorry. First I nearly walk over you, then I waste your afternoon with my angsty travelogue.'

'It's my pleasure to listen,' said Goodwin with genuine kindness. 'Why were you on the *Ilala*?'

'Last touristy thing I wanted to do before leaving Malawi. I fly back to Joburg tomorrow night. Then straight to London the next day – just for a night – then on to Tel Aviv.'

'London? Then *Tel Aviv?*'

Drew laughed. 'Ja I know it's a bit mad, and I really am going to settle down and "lead a normal life", as they say.' Drew inserted dramatic air quotes. 'Probably sooner rather than later. I'm legitimately quite keen on the whole concept of putting down roots. But this Bible I found – there's so much about Israel. And Jerusalem. I guess that's obvious. And I'm keen to see it all for myself. Where Jesus walked, and healed guys, and died. I want to take the opportunity now, while I still have my old man's credit card at my disposal.'

'Have you thanked him? I mean, for all these plane tickets?'

Goodwin's question rippled in the twilight and settled like a pebble at the bottom of Drew's soul.

'No. No I guess I haven't. Not really.'

Goodwin said nothing. Then –

'You know, I didn't go on the *Ilala*. But I went on a fishing boat with my sister and a guy she knows here. Decent guy – not one of her – you know. I'd never been on a boat and I got so sick. Straightaway – we were hardly off the beach. Over the side of the boat – chunks of my lunch. It was terrible. I feel sick in buses too. Tomorrow will be a long day. Anyway – this guy told me to look at the horizon. All the time he was saying *"Look at the horizon! Look at the horizon! Don't look down into the boat! Don't look down at the water! Keep your eyes on the horizon!"*'

'And it helped?' asked Drew.

'Yes.'

'And this has to do with me thanking my dad… how?'

'I just think – when bad stuff happens,' Goodwin went on, 'we look down into the boat and we ask *why why why*. Like, why did your dad leave? Why did *my* dad leave? Why did my sister end up here – doing this? Why has God let my country fall apart? And even yours. Or we look down at the waves rocking the boat. And all that does is make us get sick or scared and that helps no one and mostly we don't find the answers at the bottom of the boat, or the bottom of the lake, you know?'

'True story.' Drew had stretched out on the sand and was staring up at the thickening twilight's first blinking stars.

'And maybe it's then that we need to look up and we need to look far – to the horizon of history – and remember all our stories are connected by three big dots: in the beginning, meanwhile, and in the end.'

'Dots?' said Drew, intrigued.

'It's like this. In the beginning – first dot – people sinned and the world broke and that wave of sin has rolled on ever since and it's responsible for our meanwhile. That's where you are now. Me too. We're in the meanwhile. The middle dot. We're in a broken world where crazy, terrible things happen. It's not fair. It's just true. But in the *end*, God will roll up all of history for His glory. The last dot! He'll make everything new. And it takes faith but, Drew, maybe we've got to look up, and keep our eyes on the horizon – on *that* distant shore.'

Goodwin was quiet for a bit. He raked his fingers through the sand.

'We just met and maybe we don't see each other again after tomorrow's bus ride so you don't have to listen to what I say. I just want to tell you that everything's going to be ok in the end – in the *very* end, at least – and I know your dad messed up – and he messed up a lot of stuff for you – but if you stop trying to find answers in all that mess, and if you remember that eventually God will work it all out for your good and His glory, then maybe you'll be able to forgive your dad. And even say thank you for all the plane tickets.'

Drew sat up again but didn't say anything. He felt spent. And content just to breathe in the truth of Goodwin's words and gaze at the darkening horizon over the lake, and the brightening horizon of his mind. Goodwin slapped him lightly on the back and said, 'We should eat now. I'd love you to meet Aneni. Are you staying at the youth hostel? Tomorrow we brave the bus, so you can keep your appointment with Jerusalem.'

14

London

*'Where we find difficulty we may always expect that
a discovery awaits us.'*

C.S. Lewis

JD wondered how many people had sat on this seat before him. He could
tell the fabric used to be bright blue. Now it was average blue. There was
something grey – maybe chewing gum – pressed deep and immovable into
the side of the seat next to him.

He wondered what kinds of germs populated the floor. He wondered
if they thrived in vast germ cities. If there was a germ mayor, and germ
municipality officials yelling, *'Spread the muck!'* He wondered if there was a
way to enter that tiny germ world – like how the kids got into Narnia – and
he thought about how his gran had got him all seven Chronicles on Audible
and he'd listened over and over and all those stories had marvellously
climbed inside his brain the way those kids had climbed inside a cupboard.

He thought all this to the train's soundtrack… *rock-rock… tha-thwack…
rock-rock… tha-thwack…*

He decided he liked trains, germs or no germs, crammed with peak-
hour people – as this one was – or empty. Trains soothed him the way drums

did. The rhythm steadied him, and he didn't feel as if gears were slipping in his head, like he did when he couldn't read words.

His mom was drifting in and out of a doze, her head lolling against the backdrop of a black rushing tunnel. She'd brought him to London to 'visit her cousin' and 'show him the sights', but he knew they couldn't afford an overseas holiday. He knew his grandparents had paid. He knew they were here because she was thinking of moving. She reckoned the schools here could cope better with his dyslexia. He knew all this because he was thirteen and he understood the clandestine code he wasn't supposed to understand – the one she used when she spoke to other adults. He knew she didn't want to upset him until the decision was final, so he went along with the sight-seeing, family-visiting pretence.

And he had to admit, London was cool. Normally when he heard the word *museum* his brain clicked *delete* and the word fell into a tiny bin icon along with words like *test* and *homework* and *green leafy vegetables*. But some of the museums they'd visited in London seriously rocked. Plus there were the bridges and the parks and the hotdog stands and the red buses that made JD feel like he was in a movie.

He still worried though. About his mom. About whether a move would be the best thing for them. He wasn't sure she'd cope without his gran and grandpa and the friends she was finally starting to make at church. The recrimination swept across his mind like it did every day – a hideous, familiar visitor who meddled in his thoughts and no amount of drumming or train-track *tha-thwacking* could dislodge it.

It's your fault. If she didn't have you, she'd be free.

'This is us, love.'

The train was slowing and his mom was standing to gather her stuff. They were heading back to her cousin's place. Clare was four years younger than Lizette. Wise and kind in an eccentric, worldly way. JD liked her, and he liked that their touristy-day-out was over and they could look forward to whatever imaginative fusion food Clare was spicing up for them. He was spending the whole of the next day with Clare, while his mom ostensibly shopped but actually visited secondary schools and employment agencies.

They were on the silver tube line – the Jubilee line – and this was Willesden Green Station and Clare lived two blocks away. Apparently a bunch of people were also getting off here – shouldering their way towards the doors – and others were jostling on the platform to get on – and JD watched his mom edge her way to the sliding doors – *Mind the gap* – and she got wedged there for a moment in the throng and she turned back to him with a tight smile to check he'd picked up his daypack and was following her out but then a stream of people hurried into the compartment and his bag strap got caught under someone's shoe – 'Sorry sir. 'Scuse me. *Excuse me!*' – and the doors closed and the train chugged and his mom stared pale and wide-eyed from the platform and through the glass he saw her mouthing – 'No no no! JD!' – and then she was gone.

Rock-rock... tha-thwack... rock-rock... tha-thwack...

The rocking and thwacking sounded suddenly like the White Witch cackling and Aslan was nowhere and JD stopped breathing and felt sick. Then he was breathing hard and fast and gripping an overhead strap to keep from reeling and he was fighting tears and the hideous visitor in his thoughts grew loud.

Don't cry. Don't be a baby. She's gone and she's better off without you. Might as well just stay on the train.

'Hey man, was that your mom? Did you miss your stop, dude?'

JD felt a hand on his shoulder and looked up to find the owner of the South African accent. Kind eyes. JD tried to stop gasping –

'Ja – my bag got caught – I was s'posed to – '

'It's ok. It's really ok. Come, sit – there's a seat here.' JD let the guy lead him deeper into the compartment. People had settled into seats or were standing close to the doors for the next stop and the train wasn't as jammed as it had been. JD's legs went numb. He slumped into the seat.

'I'm Drew.' Drew held out a hand.

'JD.'

'Ok. Take a deep breath, dude. That's it. And another. Good.' In between gulps of air JD was struck by how unfathomably calm this guy seemed.

'Listen, your mom will know to wait for you at Willesden Green, ok?' She would, JD knew. Clare had even coached them on this stuff – about not getting rattled if they got separated because the trains could do no other than keep to their tracks and you were safe inside. 'D'you have a phone? Or does your mom have her phone on her?'

JD shook his head. 'I don't have one. And her battery died.'

'No probs. I'm getting out at Wembley Park – two stops' time. I'll see you to the other platform and make sure you get on a train, then you hop out at Willesden Green, ok? So this is not a train smash, ha ha.' He smiled and added, 'Too soon?'

JD smiled back. 'Sorry – just got a fright.'

'Of course you did.'

'My mom's super stressed. She's gonna be freaking out.' Tears pricked and he swallowed as hard as he could.

'Moms are pretty strong,' said Drew – unruffled, matter-of-fact. 'I'm sorry she's stressed. Are you guys on holiday? Is your dad around?'

JD looked at him and simultaneously said nothing, and everything.

'Sorry dude. Not my business.'

'No, it's chilled. Don't know my dad. We're staying with my mom's cousin. I think my mom wants us to move here 'cause I suck at school and I think she's hoping there's something better for me here.'

'Ah.'

'D'you live here – London?'

'No. I've been traveling the past few years. All over. So home is still officially Joburg, I guess. I'm just in London tonight, then I fly to Tel Aviv tomorrow.'

'Why?' JD blurted and felt like a toddler.

Drew smiled. 'Well, I'm in London to catch up with a friend, then I'm going to Israel. I'll head to Jerusalem from Tel Aviv.'

'Why?' *Get a grip,* screamed JD at himself in his head.

Drew answered with a question of his own. 'Do you guys go to church and stuff, at home?'

'Ja.'

'So, I want to see where Jesus walked, and died. And rose again.'

'Cool,' said JD flatly. *I wonder if Jesus ever wanted to run away,* he thought. *Because maybe, if there'd been a train, He could've stayed on it and then He needn't have died.* And the hideous visitor was back, rocking and thwacking. *She's better off without you. Stay on the train. Stay on the train. Stay on the train.*

'Do you know what happens if someone just stays on a train?' JD asked.

Drew looked at him intently. 'Yip. Shot at dawn.'

JD laughed even though it was lame. Drew was quiet for a while. Then he turned to JD and said softly, 'Dude. Don't even think about it.'

JD stared at the floor. Nodded almost imperceptibly. Then he said –

'Why not?'

'Because you've got a future,' replied Drew.

'How do you know?'

'Because you're loved.'

'How do you know?'

'Ok, man, I'm gonna speak freely,' said Drew, 'because we might not see each other again – after Wembley Park – which is the next stop.'

JD nodded again and for some reason blood rushed hot to his cheeks.

'So you know the story of Joseph, in Genesis? His brothers sell him into slavery and all, right? But then at the end the brothers feel super bad and they reckon Joseph's just gonna cancel them, one time. But he says to them, "You intended to *harm* me, but God intended it all for *good*." And it seems lousy that you got separated from your mom just now, but maybe God intended it for *good*. I can't help wondering,' said Drew, 'if God has stopped you in your tracks – ha! See what I did there? – on the Jubilee line. For a reason.'

'Why?' said JD again. 'Like I said. I suck at school. Not following.' But Drew had his attention.

'Well, *jubilee* means emancipation – like, when slaves are set free? – and restoration. And this is the *silver* line – it had something to do with Queen Elizabeth's Silver Jubilee. Twenty-five years on the throne. And – this sounds so cheesy but hear me out, brother – maybe God wants you to see there's a silver lining in your circumstances right now. And He's setting you free. And everything's going to be ok. And, this is Wembley Park. Come on.'

JD wasted no time elbowing out of the train. Drew followed a little more leisurely, his enormous backpack slung over one shoulder. JD was breathing hard again as he made his way with Drew up some stairs, across the bridge straddling the tracks, down some stairs, and onto the opposite platform where even now a train was hurtling in, eastbound for Stratford.

'Thanks Drew,' JD said, 'Sorry for panicking and all. Sorry if I've wasted your time.'

'No worries at all! It was rad to meet you,' grinned Drew. 'And I'm glad you didn't stay on the train.'

JD laughed a bit. 'Ha! I guess. Have fun on your Jesus-tour thingy.'

And Drew laughed too. 'I think I will! Remember to *get off at Willesden Green*, bru.'

The train doors hissed open – *Mind the gap* – and JD stepped onto the train. Then Drew was pulling something from his backpack on the platform and suddenly he was there again, leaning on the doors to keep them from closing.

'Take this.' Drew shoved a tattered brown leather book into JD's hands.

'Your Bible?'

Mind the gap.

'Ja, I want you to have it. Look at Psalm a hundred and thirty-eight – there's a bookmark. Some of it's highlighted. Just read it, JD. You'll see,' then, for the second time: 'Everything's going to be ok.'

The doors closed. Drew waved. JD found a seat. Magically, the hideous visitor voice was silent. He had two stops to enjoy the *rock-rock... tha-thwack...* He leant back, and breathed.

Then JD looked down at the Bible in his lap, a little starstruck, because what were the chances of a guy as cool as Drew giving him the time of day, never mind a Bible – of all things – that clearly meant a lot to him?

Psalm a hundred and thirty-eight, Drew had said. JD had a Bible at home but he'd opened it so little the pages still stuck together which made him less inclined to open it at all. The writing was practically microscopic and the words dived and swam more than ever, surfing the waves of JD's self-consciousness.

He knew from rhymes and raps Nadia had taught them at King's Kids that Psalms was somewhere in the middle. He flipped open the book. The writing was a little bigger at least.

Psalms... He paged... *One three eight.*

It was bookmarked, as Drew said it would be. An empty McDonald's salt sachet, the corner torn off, was wedged in the gutter between the pages. JD hadn't pictured Drew as someone who highlighted stuff, but every other verse of this psalm was smudged luminous green. For JD, it was awesome. The brightness and the contrast helped to settle and still the letters.

'I give You thanks, O LORD, with all my heart...' read JD, then skipped to the next highlighted bit – *'...for Your promises are backed by all the honour of Your name.'* And verse three – *'As soon as I pray, You answer me; You encourage me by giving me strength.'* And verse six – *'Though the LORD is great, He cares for the humble...'*

And then the last verse. Verse eight.

JD had heard Christians say weird things like, 'The words just leapt off the page!' It irritated him because all he wanted was for the words to stop leaping and sit still.

But on a train in London with a cool announcement airing above his head – *The next station is Willesden Green. This train terminates at Stratford* – the words on the page were motionless. He read them and re-read them and felt an immense delight blooming within.

'The LORD will work out His plans for my life – for Your faithful love, O LORD, endures forever. Don't abandon me, for You made me.'

The Lord would work out His plans for JD's life. *I have a future.*

His faithful love endured forever. *I'm loved.*

He would never abandon JD – because He was the One who'd *made* JD.

Which meant that maybe – just maybe – *I'm not a mistake.*

Not all these thoughts were lining up in JD's mind and heart in ways he could perfectly understand or accept but he considered that maybe, just maybe, even if a drunk student had half-raped another drunk student, intending to harm her – which he'd gathered (from eavesdropping, and journals he shouldn't have read) was how he'd become a human thirteen years ago – maybe God had intended it all for good? Intended *him* for good?

And then the train stopped and he yanked his bag from the floor and bounded out the doors, onto the platform and into the arms of his sobbing mom who was saying over and over how sorry she was she'd left him like that and how proud she was of him and how he'd done the right thing to catch the train back and she'd been praying and praying.

'It worked,' said JD – animated – thrilled to be safe and sound. Thrilled to be happy and free and whole and *not a mistake*. 'The praying worked.'

As the train slid on, leaving them laughing their teary relief all over the platform, no one sat in JD's still-warm seat. Just the Bible with the smooth, brown, faux leather cover.

15

London

'Life, if well lived, is long enough.'

Lucius Annaeus Seneca

'You dropped this, luv!'

Stepping from the train onto the platform at Green Park Station – *Mind the gap* – Jules turned towards the woman who'd sat next to her and felt the insistent thrust of something smooth and book-shaped into her middle with the doors already gliding closed –

'No no – it's not – '

The train began to move –

' – mine!'

Jules stood stunned – statuesque – on the platform. She stared after the quickening train. Then she stared at the leather-covered Bible that had just been shoved upon her. She guessed it must've fallen on the floor – left behind by another passenger – and the woman had spotted it as Jules alighted and assumed it was hers and felt the neighbourly thing was to return it.

Except, it didn't belong to Jules.

Oops, said Jules to Jesus in her thoughts. *Well. Is this from You? Thank You.*

Wow. Bizarre.

Jules had taken the Jubilee line from Canary Wharf where she'd spent the warm, cloudless morning meandering through slightly less tourist-infested souvenir shops and enjoying the lawns of Canada Square Park. *The thinner the crowds today, the better,* she'd thought because her head hurt.

'It's just all the traveling,' she'd told Bryce, 'and hotel mattresses.'

'Well, today is for chilling, ok? Enjoy the kid-free solitude,' Bryce had said over their hotel breakfast that morning, signalling a waiter. 'Two more coffees, please? Soon as my meetings are done, I'll get a shuttle to the airport with the bags, so you needn't come back here. Just take the tube to Heathrow and meet me there?'

'Perfect,' Jules smiled. Just before breakfast they'd FaceTimed their school-holiday-winter-pyjama-clad kids at Bryce's folks' place in Pretoria. She'd *oohed* and *aahed* at all their sweet stories and blown dozens of kisses and touched the screen – 'Last touch! Love you! Last touch!' – and then she'd had a good cry because she ached for them even though she and Bryce were having an incredible time.

They'd spent three languid days in Prague before flying to London. A maximiser who was always looking for time-and-space congruency, Bryce had tacked on the Czech Republic, and some business, to their French adventure. Today he had clients to meet, and Jules had overpriced, fluffy, Union Jack top hats to buy for the kids. Tonight, at last, they were flying to Paris. In a couple days they'd hire a car and drive to the Loire Valley to find the lavender fields Jules had long been loving through the cover of a magazine.

On the platform of Green Park Station, Jules fingered the worn cover of the unlikely, unexpected gift she'd mistakenly been given. She considered leaving it with station officials. *Surely the London Underground has a lost-and-found system,* she thought. Instead, she slipped it into her bag because it intrigued and delighted her in a Velveteen Rabbit kind of way. She could tell –

fanning through the thin pages marked with scribblings and bright shades of emphasis – this Bible had been loved so much it had almost become real. As real, she decided, as God's Word really-truly-actually was. Plus, she'd been swiping through YouVersion on her phone while they travelled, and she missed turning paper pages.

So, pleased and flummoxed, Jules rode the escalator up into the light and life of London. *So, so weird*, she kept thinking. Later she'd catch the Piccadilly line from Green Park to Heathrow, but she didn't need to do that just yet. She had time, she was hungry (*Maybe that's why I've got the headache again*, she thought), and TripAdvisor assured her there were mind-bending gourmet sandwiches to be had not far from here.

Mind-bending price, thought Jules grimly as she did the mental currency conversion and paid for a toasted ciabatta that was merely a vehicle for a mound of roasted chicken breast with candied bacon, fresh avocado, melted Swiss cheese and unidentifiable-but-almost-orgasmic sauce.

She ate on a bench in Green Park surrounded by sun-starved Britons joyfully flinging frisbees, then decided she needed to walk off the sandwich even though her jeans were a little looser since leaving home. *Thank You God*, she thought, *but how is that even possible, with everything we've been eating?* She wandered past The Ritz and took a selfie with the famously glitzy sign in the background and fantasized about being Julia Roberts in *Notting Hill*.

Her phone buzzed. A text from Beth –

Hello friend, you still having fun? You've been on my mind! Xx

Jules sent Beth the selfie, adding –

Yes! Missing the kids like mad. Serious #momguilt! But it's been amazing. Got the day to myself. Meeting Bryce at Heathrow later then to Paris we go, whoop whoop! All good your side? Lots of love!

She and Beth had grown close. In the world of white privilege and wealth they both inhabited, Jules was increasingly drawn to Beth's straight-talking authenticity and unpretentiousness – her courage not only to be comfortable with discomfort, but to turn it into a song. Beth lived an unaffected life of clear purpose and genuine humility. And she wasn't as intimidatingly perfect as Jules had first summed her up to be. Where Jules struggled to articulate her purpose, Beth never did. But where Beth's insecurities threatened to derail her, she found in Jules a grounded-ness that calmed and comforted.

Jules and Beth each had a daughter in Grade 1 at Chelsea Preparatory and they'd fallen into the easy habit of parking next to each other ten minutes before pickup in the afternoons, for a quick carpark chat.

'We're *those* moms, friend!' Jules had joked a few weeks back. She bleeped her car and joined Beth who was leaning against the passenger door of her Fortuner. 'The rumourmongering, carpark moms.'

Beth gave a sort-of smile but didn't say anything. She took off her sunglasses.

'You've been crying,' blurted Jules, stating the extremely obvious.

Beth laughed but couldn't keep her eyes from swimming. 'Ha! Yes. But at least I have tact!'

'What's going on?'

'Arg. Bad day. No big deal,' deflected Beth unconvincingly and Jules gave her The Look so Beth said, 'Ok ok. I'll tell you. It's just silly though. I feel like such a child,' and she rubbed a hand across her face and sighed.

'I just put on lip gloss in the car,' countered Jules, 'because I'm feeling frumpy in these *designer* tracksuit pants from Ackermans and I'm terrified I run into fearsome Principle Rodgers who disparagingly sucks in her perfectly contoured cheekbones when she sees me, like I'm a dishrag sullying her pristine corridors. I'm safe. You can tell me.'

124

Beth laughed properly this time. 'It's just that – well, I've hit another hundred thousand downloads of *Breath of God* – '

'*Your breath gives me life, Almighty Redeemer,*' sang Jules. 'Had it stuck in my head all day. But in the good way! Not the irritating way. I can't get enough of it. It's becoming a bit of an anthem for me. I *love* it.'

'Thanks friend,' smiled Beth. 'It's just that, some of my closest friends – not you, evidently – and even my family – they *don't* love it. They don't listen. Not to anything I say or sing. It keeps my feet on the ground, that's for sure. Every time I think I'm some kind of awesome, I go, "Well, I can't be *that* awesome because the people who've known me longest and deepest can't even – I don't know – hear my voice?"' Beth sighed and rolled her eyes. 'I told you this was childish. I can totally hear how ridiculous – and narcissistic – it sounds when I say it out loud, but when the people who are actually *in* my life – the people I'm in relationship with – when they – '

'Can't see the beautiful wood because they're standing too close to this little tree?'

'I guess.' Beth nodded and sighed. 'It's like, if my brother's wife – or a friend from high school – if they would just *like* one of my Instagram stories – just once – it would make my decade.'

Jules was quiet. Beth said, 'Gosh, sorry, friend. I'm pretty amazed at my shallowness too, trust me. I know all the theology on this – you know, finding my security in Christ blah blah. I've written *lyrics* about this stuff. And I've got all these followers looking to me for answers, and I'm pathetic.'

'You're not shallow or pathetic,' said Jules. 'Well. Maybe you're a *little* shallow and pathetic.'

'Wow,' Beth cracked up, 'With friends like you…'

Jules grinned at her. 'We're all a little shallow and pathetic. But you need to stop beating yourself up about this, Beth. I get it. You don't need fans. You need friends. Because we're made for community, not fame. Also, we *need* validation and encouragement. Underneath pretending to adult, we all just feel like kids, right? And we all just want the *well-done*, the *you're-enough*, the *love* of a Heavenly Father. We're wired for it. And, #obviously, in our stupid, sinful, limited human way, we look for that affirmation from other people, instead of finding it in Him. Good grief, I mean, I'm looking for validation from Mrs Rodgers, and seriously, why should I care if she thinks I'm sophisticated enough to be a mom at her school?'

'Your lip gloss *is* pretty great,' said Beth.

'I know, right?' They were both laughing. 'But listen,' continued Jules, 'There could be a dozen reasons why these peeps are being un-generous with their follows or their feedback. Most of those reasons probably say more about them than they say about you and all those reasons are none of your business. They're between those people, and God. What *is* your business, is obedience.'

'You're pretty wise for someone wearing tracksuit pants from Ackermans.'

'Preach!'

'So what do you think obedience means – in this?' asked Beth.

'Well, you know in Thessalonians somewhere Paul says something like, *"Make it your ambition to lead a quiet life."* I reckon that's pretty much it.'

'Oh gosh. That is so hard.' Beth sighed and stared at her feet. 'I don't even know how to start leading a quiet life. Most of my life happens behind a microphone.'

'Maybe,' said Jules, 'it's asking God for the courage to keep being kind, even though others aren't being kind to you – at least, they're not being kind in the way you'd like them to be kind. Because it's possible they have no idea it's what you need from them, you know? It's possible they think there isn't space for them in your public profile. It's possible they're jealous. That's *definitely* not your problem. Just be kind. Put your head down and carry on doing what God has called you to do. Keep writing your songs, and keep singing them. Keep speaking. And do it for His glory, not yours. And listen for His quiet *well done*, in the moments no one else will ever see or know about. Also, just so you know,' Jules bumped her elbow against Beth's, 'I'm in your corner.'

Standing in front of The Ritz texting Beth, Jules thought back to that conversation, and how the people who need encouragement the most are those who look as if they need it the least. Even Julia Roberts in *Notting Hill*. And she thought about how she needed to take her own advice. She needed to make it her ambition to lead a quiet life. Put her head down and obey God's call on her life in this season – wife, mom, distributor of Lunchbox Luxuries – regardless of who did or didn't understand or notice or applaud her. She needed to listen for the quiet *well done* – and trust Him for the rest.

Of late Jules had been unusually *thinkative*. She wondered if she shouldn't be *writing down* all the thinkative thoughts somewhere, for future thinkative thinkers, because her brain seemed bent on confirming her beliefs and consolidating her experiences into something of a life thesis. God was bringing a holy clarity to waters muddied for decades by the opinions of others. *Maybe this is just what happens when you're turning forty in a year's time,* she thought.

And with all these thinkative thoughts still in mind Jules made her way back to Green Park Station. She boarded the westbound Piccadilly line for Heathrow Terminal 5 – 'Where dreams go to die,' Bryce always joked – and settled into a seat, remembering the night at 9th Avenue Waterside when Bryce had set *this* dream aflame.

She thought how a rare moment alone on a train could feel like a golden gift to a woman so used to her boobs being elbowed by wrestling kids at bedtime. She thought about how sometimes it felt like no part of her was sacred – her whole body given over as it was to loving her family and how it left her feeling disoriented sometimes but she wouldn't want it any other way because mostly she felt spent and stretched to a satisfying fullness – like *this was the life!* And maybe the disoriented feeling had more to do with the headaches she'd been getting because if she were totally honest, they'd started before this trip.

She thought about how odd it was that weekly, in the bathroom mirror, she discovered faint new paths on her face's wrinkle roadmap, and yet she still felt sexy, but with a better idea of what to do with it. She felt like a woman who still had the hopes and dreams of a girl. On her last birthday she'd felt as if she were *growing older*, not *getting old*. Her years were filling up with life, not seeping away.

She thought about the global litter campaign she hadn't accomplished.

She thought about the dress she'd bought in Prague, for dinner in the Old Town overlooking the Vltava River. Her mom was still the voice in her head and she'd heard it: *Mutton dressed up as lamb.* She'd bought the dress anyway, to stand in solidarity with her autonomous, grownup self. She thought about how she would be the voice in her kids' heads one day and how she didn't feel like enough of an autonomous grownup to be shaping the worldview of other humans.

All this made her feel a bit lost. And her bag felt a bit heavy.

The Bible.

She'd forgotten it, but now she reached for it and rested it on her lap as the train swished on. She fanned the pages again, forming an old school, kaleidoscope animation with the highlighted bits. She flicked to the gospel of John because it was her favourite. John had been Jesus' very good friend, apparently, and she wanted that kind of intimacy with Him too.

John six. Jesus, the Bread of Life.

Familiar, comforting verses. Then verses thirty-nine and forty – and she knew Jesus was speaking straight to her slightly-lost self –

'And this is the will of God, that I should not lose even one of all those He has given Me, but that I should raise them up at the last day. For it is my Father's will that all who

128

see His Son and believe in Him should have eternal life. I will raise them up at the last day.'

Not lost, she marvelled gratefully. *Raised up.* There was still a dull thudding in her head – not helped by the subtle swaying of the train. She shifted in her seat and the movement flipped back the Bible's pages – and she was in Isaiah thirty. She glanced down at verse fifteen because it was highlighted in pink.

'This is what the Sovereign LORD, the Holy One of Israel, says: "Only in returning to Me and resting in Me will you be saved. In quietness and confidence is your strength…"'

Jules closed her eyes and leant her head against the train's window. She thought about how her life, like every human life, was an unfinished symphony but that really, all her dreams had pretty much come true. If another good thing never happened to her – ever again – for as long as she lived – that was ok. She had Jesus, and Jesus was enough. She smiled. *In quietness and confidence,* she thought. *I'm good with that, God.*

16

Jerusalem

*'One doesn't go to Jerusalem; one returns to it.
That's one of its mysteries.'*

Elie Wiesel

The cashier looked down at the pink lip balm Drew slid across the counter.
Then he glanced at Drew. Then back at the lip balm.

'You want this one?' he said, in the heavily accented English of Israel.
'This one – is for the ladies? Is strawberry ice.' The guy's smile was hidden
beneath an enormous black moustache, but Drew knew when he was being
mocked.

He was tired from half a week's worth of traveling – from Monkey
Bay to Blantyre to Johannesburg to London to Tel Aviv – and finally to
Jerusalem. He'd slept fitfully, and not enough, even when he was horizontal
under sheets and not in a bus or a plane or an airport lounge. He was acutely
aware there wasn't a bed in the world that felt like his. His mom had even
replaced the mattress on the bed he'd grown up sleeping in, in his bedroom
in Houghton.

Arriving in Jerusalem just before midday, he'd checked into an ancient
building that housed a clean and comfortable hostel, between the Jewish

and Armenian Quarters in the Old City. He laid claim to a bunk but didn't try it out. Just dumped his backpack and headed out for food. And lip balm. Because even though he was hardcore, dry lips were the pits and he was out of Zam-Buk and he knew he couldn't start enjoying himself until his lips stopped burning.

He gave the cashier a weary smile. 'Yes please. It's fine.' It wasn't as if this pharmacy – which had taken him the better part of an hour to find in the labyrinth of Old City streets – had a plethora of masculine-looking lip balm options. Also, it wasn't as if there was any English on the packaging. It was pink. There was a big-lipped grinning strawberry wearing sunglasses. That seemed fine.

'I see yes,' the cashier winked knowingly, 'Is *for the ladies.*'

Whatever, thought Drew.

He reached for his wallet which triggered thoughts of his dad. Since Malawi – and specifically, since he'd almost stepped on the nice Zimbabwean on the lake beach that day – Drew's ruminations about his dad centred increasingly on his dad's generosity. His dad had botched things royally in almost every area of his life. Still, there was no denying he'd been generous.

How much more, he heard the question in his thoughts, *how much more generous is your Father in heaven?*

Drew paid for the stick of pink strawberry ice – 'Enjoy,' the cashier winked again – and Drew turned around – looking down – and walked straight into the woman behind him who had simultaneously turned towards the throat lozenges on a shelf near the till and Drew didn't quite knock her over but he did send flying the box of tampons and the shower gel she'd been about to pay for.

What is with *me, and walking into people?* Drew yelled into the confusion of his thoughts.

'Oh my word I'm so sorry – sorry – let me get that,' he said out loud, still not looking up but definitely *blushing* of all the stupid things to be doing as he reached for the tampons – *regular flow*, he noted – and then he heard laughter and he finally looked up, and she was there.

And he couldn't speak.

She was still laughing.

'It's ok,' she said. 'No worries. Just an accident.'

He still couldn't speak. He still clung to the tampons. He was staring at her – registering every detail – jeans, green Jeep t-shirt, tan ankle boots – and he was sure she must be waiting for someone in a white coat to lead him gently away with apologetic backward glances at the pharmacy staff and patrons. (*'So sorry, folks. We're just going to take Drew back to the Home for a nice cup of tea. He gets a little overwhelmed in pharmacies, don't you Drew?'*)

Now she was really laughing – and holding out a hand – waiting for him to hand over the box. 'They're just tampons. For that whole "menstrual cycle" thing?' Drew's mouth was hanging open. *Stop staring!* He silently berated himself again, staring. 'Shockingly,' she went on when he still didn't relinquish the box, 'it happens to almost fifty percent of the world's population, every month.'

And finally, something that was almost Drew's normal laugh surfaced and they both stood up – but he still couldn't stop staring, because, *it was her*.

'I'm sorry – again, for bashing into you – but also, have we met?'

'Are you serious right now?' she had the full-on giggles.

'Ah man. That's not a pickup line,' he was cracking up too. 'You should probably pay for that.' He stood aside and she handed over cash and avoided eye contact with black-moustache man who had witnessed – and evidently enjoyed – the entire fiasco.

'You're, um, obviously South African too? And far from Joburg,' she was still laughing. 'But no, I doubt we've met.' She was shoving her purchases into a red daypack as they headed out the pharmacy together. 'I'm Thandeka.'

'Drew.' They shook hands awkwardly and Drew tried to control the size of his smile. *Be cool, be cool, be cool,* he said over and over to his spinning, sweating mind-body-soul.

'What, um, brings you to the pharmacy? I mean Jerusalem. I mean, are you traveling or like – '

Thandeka was the one staring now. 'Ok…' she said, 'What I know for sure is that I'm hungry, and the best falafel in the history of humans is from that guy.' She pointed across the cobbled alleyway to a hole-in-the-wall joint that looked suspiciously filthy but smelled unbelievable.

'Thank God,' said Drew sincerely, visibly relaxing. 'I'm in.' He had the spinning and the sweating ever so slightly under control. 'It's on me. Least I can do.'

They crossed the street, sat down on plastic garden furniture, and immediately two glasses of steaming peppermint tea were placed on the table between them and for the first time that day, it dawned on Drew that he was *here*, the *genius loci* of an ancient city seeping into his own spirit, gentle and strong with spice and history and holiness. *Jerusalem.*

'Mmm,' Drew took a sip and raised polite eyebrows of appreciation in the direction of the smiling proprietor who introduced himself as Amir and stood grinning manically at the two of them, clasping his hands in glee. They ordered two falafels in pita and Amir sprang into action behind his counter.

'Tastes like hot toothpaste,' rasped Drew, generously applying his new pink lip balm. 'Also, I don't remember ordering tea?'

'It's a sign of hospitality,' laughed Thandeka. 'You're going to have to down a little more, or Amir might spit in your hummus.'

'What?'

'Kidding!' she hadn't really stopped laughing since Drew had bashed into her, and that made him like her even more and he wished he'd made time for a decent haircut in Joburg or London but then again, *was this even really happening* because he *knew* he'd seen her – met her – or had he?

'So, you asked what brought me to Jerusalem. I'm a flight attendant and – '

'Yes! *Yes!* That's it! I knew it!' Drew was just about levitating – tea splashed all over his jeans. 'Ow.'

'And… you're hilarious. And very strange,' laughed Thandeka.

'Oh my freakin' word. Look, I'm not usually – not *ever* – like this, ok? You have to believe me,' Drew's smile was leaning towards uncontrollable again. 'But we *have* met. Ok no. That's not true. We didn't *actually* meet. But I saw you. At the airport. Montreal. April last year.'

'What?' Thandeka was just about bent double with laughter now. 'Dude I think that lip balm is stronger than it looks – '

'You were getting out of a hotel shuttle and I was waiting to get in. You obviously had a flight – you were all, like, stunning and glowing – kind of like now – but in uniform – clearly stunning and glowing is just what you look like – but you didn't even look at me – and normally if women *aren't* in a rush they look at me – I'm just saying – so I knew you were rushing – '

'Oh wow,' said Thandeka, whose smile also seemed a little unhinged, 'You *are* sure of yourself.' She looked up, scanning the landscape of her mind for the memory. 'April. I remember that day – that flight – *gosh*. But ja, I definitely don't remember you.'

Drew looked briefly crestfallen and she laughed again. 'It's ok – I do believe you! I just don't remember you. But wow. You, um, you have a good memory. Obviously.'

'Well. You made an impression. Obviously.' They were looking into each other's eyes now and suddenly Drew's universe stopped spinning completely and he was fixed entirely on Thandeka and she was the one rendered briefly speechless.

She certainly had made an impression. For more than a year, on and off, in his dreams and random recollections, the image of her had drifted into Drew's thoughts: a drop-dead gorgeous flight attendant stepping out of a shuttle. A woman he – crazily, nonsensically, irrationally – somehow knew he could love.

Amir cleared his throat.

'Oh! Yum. Great. Thanks!' said Drew a little too enthusiastically, the reverie broken. Thandeka didn't lift her eyes from the table, smiling into the fragrant, falafel-stuffed pita breads Amir placed on the table.

'Ok,' said Drew, enjoying the fact that he once again felt almost entirely in control of all his limbs, 'pretend I didn't blurt all that out. Pretend we really just met. Because I guess we did only – *really* – just meet. You were saying. You're a flight attendant.' He took a bite. 'Incredible,' he managed, staring wide-eyed at the massive pita bread he clutched.

'Ja, so, a bunch of us got emails a month ago. Retrenched.'

'Woah!' Drew looked shocked.

'No, it's fine. It's kind of a blessing. An answer to prayer. If you're into that?' she looked up at him, the question in her eyes.

'I'm into that,' said Drew.

'Cool,' she smiled. 'Well, I'd been thinking of moving on anyway. I've been flying for almost a decade and I'm kinda over it, you know. I mean, it's been amazing. I've seen the world. But I've got other dreams too and, well, maybe God's taken the decision to move on out of my hands – by literally moving me on.'

'I get it,' said Drew between mouthfuls, his eyes not leaving her face. He really did get it. God was moving him on too. 'So what's the dream?'

'Preschool, I think.'

'Preschool? Wow, good for you! Will they let you use the jungle gyms though? Those things sometimes have height restrictions.'

She balled up a saucy serviette and threw it at him.

'Sorry, carry on.' They were both laughing again.

'*Teach* preschool. That's the dream. I think. Actually, that's the first time I've said it out loud. So, "tread softly because you tread on my dreams."'

'Jeepers. Yeats. You've *definitely* got more than a preschool education.'

'I loved my English teacher in high school.'

'Me too,' nodded Drew.

'Anyway, the airline said they wouldn't pay us out for leave not taken. We had to take it. So I've taken it – ta-da! And Jerusalem was one place I hadn't been. It's been pretty much – um – ' Thandeka's eyes filled with sudden tears and Drew decided he was officially, completely, in love with her – 'life changing. And I leave tomorrow morning.'

'*Tomorrow morning?*'

She laughed. 'Gee sorry! I'm spending three days in France – another crazy dream I guess.'

'Tell me.'

'Well – I lead the cabin crew on most flights now, so I don't have to do this anymore – but I used to have to tuck the inflight magazine and the puke bag into every seat pouch. And years ago, there was this one edition. The destination picture on the cover was of lavender fields in the south of France. And it said something cheesy, like, *Find your freedom.* I would look at that picture on hundreds of magazines every day for a month. For some reason I've never forgotten how it made me feel. I was so trapped, you know? But I'm not trapped anymore. I'm free.' She laughed and lifted her arms in an exaggerated stretch. 'It's all God. The past year or so, I feel like I can *breathe.* And so, France – and finding those fields – it just feels like something I need to do. Kind of like my little thanksgiving declaration of freedom.' She was suddenly overcome with post-overshare awkwardness. 'Is that as lame as it sounds?'

'*Lame?*' said Drew gobsmacked and serious. 'Can I come?'

Thandeka laughed again. 'No. You absolutely cannot come. It's something I need to do – just me. Plus, there's the fact that I've known you for – ' she glanced at her phone – 'an hour. And there's a strong chance you're a stalker.' But her smile was soft. 'I'll fly to Joburg from Paris, but I'm not working that flight. Then, I have four flights scheduled – just the Joburg-Frankfurt run, twice over – then it's officially career-game-over.'

'And then? Back home?'

'No,' said Thandeka and Drew tried hard not to look disappointed. 'I've got an ex-colleague in Atlanta. She's studying teaching through a community college there and it sounds cool. I've saved a chunk of money. And I could room with her, and look for something part-time. I miss my cousins, my *gogo*, but I'm not quite ready for home.' And suddenly she wondered if *gogo* would be ok with her bringing home a white boy. She'd never wondered that about any of the other white boys she'd been with, because she'd known she'd never be taking them home. So why him? The thought alarmed her because this white boy did seem a little unstable. And a little irresistible.

They finished their food ('Do you *ever* chew, or do you just inhale?' she teased), bought iced waters, thanked Amir, and wandered out into the narrow street, teeming now with afternoon shoppers and tour guides hustling elderly German couples out of the summer swelter and into air-conditioned buses.

'So, I just arrived,' said Drew. 'And apparently I only have you for another half a day –'

'You *have* me, do you?' she interrupted.

Drew smiled and pretended he hadn't heard her. 'So I need you please to take me to your favourite place in Jerusalem. Right now.'

Thandeka stopped abruptly. Spun on her heels and started walking briskly down the street in the opposite direction.

'Thandeka!' Drew caught hold of her hand. 'Hey! I'm sorry. I didn't mean to boss you around. We can go wherever you want. Or I can leave you alone forever. Of course, then my tragic and untimely death would be your fault.'

She was smiling. 'No one is dying tragically. It's this way. My favourite place in Jerusalem. You coming?' And she didn't pull her hand away and Drew couldn't feel his legs again.

'You never told me what brought you to Jerusalem,' she said. So as they weaved through ageless streets Drew gave her the fifteen-minute summary of his life, and his new-ish love for Jesus, and how he wanted to see for himself where Jesus died. Where he was buried. Where the women had seen the stone rolled away.

'You'll like my favourite place,' said Thandeka. 'Also, you never told me *your* crazy dreams. Which is unfair because I blabbed all of mine.'

Drew told her about the architecture positions he was thinking of applying for, in South Africa. He wanted to see real things built – real relationships too. He wanted to contribute. He wanted to stop running. He told her about a German philosopher who said that architecture was frozen music and he'd never understood that until Malawi when he heard people singing in a church he'd designed and helped to build.

'But first I'm going to Australia. I think I've finally forgiven my dad. But I want to thank him. In person.'

Thandeka listened quietly, leading Drew through Damascus Gate and out of the Old City. 'We're here,' she said.

Drew stopped. Wonderstruck. They'd come to the entrance of the Garden Tomb. *So this is the small spot on the planet You chose to conquer death*, he said silently to Jesus.

'It's free to get in, but they rely on donations, so maybe afterwards we can – '

'Absolutely,' said Drew.

They wandered into a quiet, clean-swept, flowered garden, past small clusters of tourists, and sat down on the stone wall facing a doorway hewn out of rock. A wooden sign on the door covering the tomb read, *He is not here – for He is risen.*

For a long time, they sat in silence. Thandeka glanced at Drew. Tears dripped from his very handsome jawline.

Finally, she asked, 'How did you know?'

'Know what?' Drew managed, pulling himself together. 'That I wanted to marry you? Well – '

'Oh stop it!' she whispered. 'This is holy ground!'

'Exactly.'

'I meant, how did you know Jesus was *really* real? What made you give your life to Him?'

'Sorry. I knew what you meant,' Drew admitted. 'I guess God had been nudging for a while. Then there was a night in Canada when I couldn't deny His presence anymore, and the power of His Word, and His very real involvement in the details. Actually – how weird is this – it was later that night – the night I saw you in Montreal.' And he added dramatically, 'Girl, you're my destiny. Don't fight it.'

Thandeka rolled her eyes and shook her head. Drew grinned and continued.

'Anyway, as I started reading the Bible more, and listening more – listening for the first time to what Christians were saying and listening to what God seemed to be pressing into my mind – I got it – this truth that He wasn't scared of my imperfections. In fact, He was *running towards* me in all my messed-up depravity. I felt like I was being swept off my feet by love. Kind of like now,' he said because he couldn't let slip the opportunity to flirt, 'but in a cosmic sense. And then when God finally set my feet back on the ground, I knew I'd never walk the same way. I don't know how else to explain it except that it felt like I could stand up straighter. And bend more easily towards the ideal – towards God's best for me. I felt like I'd lost the scoliosis of my rebellion.'

Now it was Thandeka who had tears dripping off her face. 'You're very poetic,' she said.

'You're very beautiful,' he said. 'And for you? How did you meet Him?'

'I'd stopped dreaming, and He met me there.'

'What do you mean – stopped dreaming?'

'I was ashamed, I guess. Ashamed of things I'd done and not done, and I just didn't see a way out of the worthlessness, so I figured, why even dream? But then God started speaking to me – like you, also through the Bible because this guy I sort of knew – long story – randomly gave me a Bible one day. And – also like you – I started learning to listen more, when He speaks to me in my mind, or heart, or whatever.'

Drew nodded. Thandeka continued –

'It's like, I'll be thinking or praying, and then all the noise in my head goes quiet and one clear sentence drops into my brain. I can almost see the letters lining up in order. And anyway, Jesus healed me – restored me – to the point where I think I'm free to dream again, you know? I'm also ok to accept that *His* dreams for my life are way better than *my* dreams for my life.'

'Precisely,' said Drew seriously. 'I bet you didn't dream you'd be knocked over in a pharmacy, and now just look at us!'

'Oh my word,' she looked skyward again as if imploring the heavens for help but couldn't keep from smiling. 'Anyway, I definitely can't always see what God's doing. I get that dreams mostly grow in the dark. But I know He's always growing something, and I know He'll do it. He'll accomplish His purposes for me.'

Drew and Thandeka spent the rest of the afternoon like this – flirting, talking, dreaming, laughing, questioning. There was the predictable exchanging of numbers and email addresses and social media handles, all while calmly pretending that an insane chemistry had not exploded between them in a matter of hours.

They left the Garden Tomb before sunset and walked and talked and bought supper near the Western Wall where orthodox Jewish men murmured sincere prayers while assiduously ignoring the inconvenient truth that they were flanked by tourists taking sacrilegious selfies. They walked and talked some more through Jaffa Gate where they bought coffees. They walked and talked towards midnight and finally, it was time to say goodbye.

They stood grinning at each other outside Thandeka's hotel. Drew looked at the ground then took hold of Thandeka's hands and said, 'You know, they say that ninety percent of couples who are introduced by a mutual friend stay together forever.'

Thandeka cracked up. 'Did you just make that up?'

'Yes.'

'And who is our mutual friend?'

'Jesus.'

Thandeka was quiet. She'd hinted un-seriously, flirtatiously, about staying in touch. Drew had hinted seriously about being the father of her children. She was equal parts terrified and electrified.

Eventually she looked at Drew, and found her voice. 'I don't know what all this means – and where we're going – *if* we're going – '

'That's ok,' he smiled.

'I'm just glad you bought that lip balm,' she said.

'Why's that?'

'Because I think you should kiss me.'

And so, he did.

How he got back to his hostel was anyone's guess. He was greeted by a profusely apologising, exhausted American gap-year student manning the late-night reception desk.

'Bro, I'm so sorry,' he said to Drew. 'We've moved you onto the roof. A tour group from Argentina arrived – their hotel booking had fallen through – I think? I couldn't actually understand what their whole deal was but we had to squeeze them into the dorm you were in – and it's pretty crowded. So I took your stuff up onto the roof. No charge for tonight. And no one else is up there so – '

'Fantastic,' smiled Drew. 'Perfect. Thanks.'

The American kid looked briefly confused, having expected disgruntlement on some level.

'Cool,' he called after Drew, who was already taking the stairs two at a time.

Drew's thoughts were racing – his senses saturated with Thandeka. He fully expected to be wide awake all night. Yet, alone on a thin mattress laid out on a flat concrete slab beneath the stars and above the lights of a sacred city, for the first time in a long time, he slept.

17

Amboise

*'I could not quiet that pearly ache in my heart that
I diagnosed as the cry of home.'*

Pat Conroy

Bryce and Jules stayed in a guesthouse in Rue Saint-Merri – between the
Centre Pompidou and the Seine. They didn't stay for breakfast.

'We'll buy *pains au chocolat* at that bakery near Pont Notre-Dame – what
d'you think?' said Bryce.

'I think abso-freakin'-lutely,' said Jules.

And with hot pastries crumbling all over the hired car, they left Paris
and took the backroads to the Loire Valley, and the lavender.

'I want to roam,' Jules said. 'I don't want to rush.' She felt a bizarre
urgency to slow everything down. She didn't want to miss a moment of this
unfolding dream.

And so it was some four hours later that they pulled into the drive of
Hôtel Le Clos d'Amboise.

'Amboise, Amboise, *Amboise*,' Jules murmured. 'It's such a lovely name
to say.'

'Jules, Jules, Jules,' said Bryce. 'Even lovelier.' He leant towards her from his left-hand-drive seat – which still felt weird – and kissed her cheek. 'We're here. Let's unpack, and eat something? My *pain au chocolat* is a thing of the distant past. Then let's find you some fields.'

Even to Jules's untrained ear, the mellifluous French of the Loire Valley was a welcome relief from the harsh Parisian accent. They were shown politely, discreetly, to their suite – a tasteful mix of elegant and homely – by soft-spoken hotel staff. They snacked from the fruit basket and lathered butter on crackers.

'This is lunch enough for me,' said Jules. She ran a hand through her hair and sighed. 'Is it weird that I want to take a bath before we go out again? I feel sticky and tired. Neck's a bit stiff. And my head's shtill thumping.'

'*Shtill?*' laughed Bryce.

Jules stared at him. 'Did I – ?' She looked confused. Then – 'Just a bit sore. I'll take a Myprodol.' She managed a smile.

Worry flicked across Bryce's face. He took a breath – self-corrected – and said brightly, 'Enjoy your soak. We're on holiday. No hurry.'

Jules hardly complained, but Bryce knew her headaches had been getting worse.

And did she really just slur her speech?

Twenty minutes later, having luxuriated in a clawfoot tub, Jules emerged with a little more colour in her cheeks. 'Ah! I feel fantastic,' she said. She rummaged happily in their suitcase for clean jeans and a shirt – 'Creased. Oh well.' – then announced she was ready to take a million photos of lavender fields.

They drove along the D952 towards Tours, then back towards Blois. They pulled over onto farm roads and cycle tracks wherever beauty apprehended them. They stopped to buy cheese. They stopped to drink coffee. They stopped for supper (and sparkling water) in Candé-sur-Beuvron. They drove and drove and the summer sun looked ready to rest and finally Jules said: 'Here!'

They had crested a gentle hill and before them sprawled a panorama of purple and green. Jules leapt from the car like their daughter Mia always did, laughing out loud as she half-skipped, half-jogged between the lavender rows.

Bryce caught up, grinning. He'd done it. They had dived into that magazine cover and were walking around inside it.

'Oh my word, oh my word, oh my word!' said Jules laughing and running her hands over the lavender and turning to Bryce – 'It's like that scene in *Gladiator* when Russell Crowe walks through the wheat, remember?'

'Smile,' said Bryce, unnecessarily. Her cheeks were aching from uninterrupted beaming. He held his phone aloft to capture the setting sun, the flowers, his Jules. Then they took far too many selfies and laughed hysterically because some of them were *so* bad and at last they stood quietly and watched the glowing embers of the evening slip silent past the horizon.

'Do you think – ' Jules began but the words caught in her throat.

'What, love?' Bryce glanced at her and the worry was back, gnawing just a little at his gut.

'Do you think I've done enough? Like, do you think I've got enough to show for my years on earth? I mean, so far. Because, #midlifecrisis.'

Bryce forced a laugh. 'Are you kidding? Yes! And also, you're just getting started! Jules, we're not even halfway through our lives! Our generation – we're probably going to live to be, like, a hundred!' He took hold of her with exaggerated enthusiasm and kissed her hair and tried to hang onto the happy, giddy delirium they'd succumbed to because it stopped the worry from taking another bite. 'You're a freakin' hero. Wife, mom, entrepreneur. Incredible in bed.'

Jules raised sexy eyebrows at him, laughed, and lightened a little.

'Also, last night I was reading a bit of first Thessalonians, in your new Bible you got by mistake – though it's pretty old I reckon? – and Paul says how we should make it our ambition to lead a quiet life. And I just thought of you, babe, because you're all about bringing your best self to everything you do, without ever asking for recognition or credit. And seriously, that makes you, like, the *most* successful human. The way you're always so present to the moment – you've achieved the height of ambition. Because the present – right here right now – that's where the magic happens.'

'Thank you,' whispered Jules, amazed to hear her own advice circling back the way, she'd learned, it inevitably did when lives were lived in healthy community. 'Thanks, my love, for saying that, and for all of this, and for loving me so well.' That morning, amidst the plush pillows of their Paris guesthouse bed, she'd also flipped through the mystery Bible she'd already lovingly possessed as her own, and come across something else Paul had written, this time to Timothy: *'And the good deeds done in secret will someday come to light.'*

The words came back to her now in the twilight, and a soft and heavy satisfaction settled over her – as if she'd fallen asleep on God's couch after a full day of life and He was spreading a thick blanket of peace over her and kissing her on the forehead.

Then she fell asleep – for real – in the car on the way back to Amboise, stirring to lean heavily on Bryce as he led her, chuckling, back to their room.

'Jus' gotta brush my teeth,' she said, falling onto their bed, eyes already closing.

Bryce laughed again. One night of unbrushed teeth never killed anyone. He stood staring down at his sleeping wife. Then it was he who covered and kissed her, profoundly grateful that he (and God, who was entirely responsible for arranging the sunset and getting all that lavender to grow) had managed to pull off her dream. Done and dusted.

The next morning, back in their room after croissants and coffee in the hotel dining room, they FaceTimed the kids. Then Bryce plugged in headphones and struck up a conference call with some Joburg clients and Jules put on her running shoes even though she knew she'd just be walking.

'I won't be long,' mouthed Bryce above his laptop screen.

Jules smiled and gave him a thumbs up, holding up her phone and a map of Amboise she'd picked up at reception and mouthed back, 'I'm going to walk to the castle. See you later.'

Bryce winked, echoed her thumbs up and blew exaggerated kisses in her direction. She stifled a laugh, gesticulated at his screen, and mouthed back, 'Behave!'

Her head ached but the day was perfect and the Château Royal d'Amboise wasn't far at all. She walked slowly, inhaling the foreign aromas of a French town in the height of summer. The rich wafting from every *pâtisserie* and *confiserie* and *boulangerie* made her queasy – almost dizzy – but nothing would cloud her contentment.

She reached the chateau and stood in line with a dozen or so other tourists – it was early still – paid her entrance fee and stepped into the ancient royal courts.

She didn't feel like going inside just yet. She gazed at the magical view of the Loire, enjoyed by French kings for centuries. All those kings were dead and gone and here she was wandering unhurriedly – *with the King of kings*, she thought – along the gardens' gravel pathways. *Bryce would call this a glacial pace*, she said to God in her thoughts, running her hands along still more lavender – and salvias and geraniums and white roses – and she was happy.

Breathlessly happy.

She didn't feel like talking to the other tourists. Like that nice girl there. South African too. Young. Beautiful.

So sore. Her head was so sore.

She stopped. Seized by nausea. Bent double. So sore. *So sore.*

'Ma'am? Ma'am are you ok?' A hand on her back. It was the pretty South African. But Jules couldn't see her now. Couldn't see.

'Can't sh-shee. Can't – '

Jules knew she was falling but couldn't feel the small stones that cut her palms and knees. All she felt was the blanket again. The God-blanket. The peace.

She thought how wonderful it was that there was so little litter in France and the words spun weirdly through her brain – *little litter little litter*.

She thought of Bryce. She knew he didn't like marmalade but he'd slap it on his toast anyway and wink at her and go *mmm…* because she'd made the marmalade and he loved her so much. So much.

She thought, *Mia-David-Leila*, her three precious babies swelling synonymously to flood out every other thought as the abyss of her love for them swallowed her and she knew there was *grace-grace-grace* for their journeys which had only just begun. Just as there had been grace for her journey which she suddenly knew was ending because, *I'm just a breath. Just a breath.*

And then the words she'd read before breakfast rose in her semi-consciousness – *Ecclesiastes something verse something?* –

'Yet God has made everything beautiful for its own time. He has planted eternity in the human heart, but even so, people cannot see the whole scope of God's work from beginning to end.'

Can't see, she thought. *Can't speak*, she thought, trying. *But all beautiful. God's work. Beginning to end.*

Jesus. Jesus.

She wanted to see Him. She knew He was close.

And then her heart's last beat knocked on the door of home.

***

The ensuing days were a haze, and Bryce wouldn't remember much of how he survived them.

But he would remember sauntering out of the hotel to catch up with Jules at the castle – and the concierge at reception – phone in hand – staring stricken: '*Monsieur. Votre femme.*'

He would remember what it felt like when the bottom dropped out of his life. The terrifying, agonizing shock and fear and loneliness rolling over him in steady waves of grief that drew back and left him numb before rolling over him again.

He would remember their last evening together because he'd left his soul in those lavender fields and he would remember the call to his parents and he would remember trying to keep his own hysteria under control as he explained to the kids that Mommy was gone.

He would remember only brief, dreadful moments of the coroner's post-mortem monologue, delivered to Bryce in English via a bored-looking social worker who kept glancing at her phone and clearly had more interesting things to do than to tell a tourist his wife's brain aneurysm was a long time coming.

He would try to forget the ghastly, practical, clinical logistics of flying a body across the world.

He wouldn't remember much of the flight home – only that he was bumped to first class though he didn't ask or care why. He would remember sitting near a young black woman – gentle – lovely. A frequent flyer because she seemed to know the flight attendants and she kept getting up and bringing him things like bottled water and hot towels and again he didn't ask or argue. And sometime in the night when the weeping overtook him, he knew she was praying.

September
2 0 1 8

*'How wonderful it is that nobody need wait a single moment
before beginning to improve the world.'*

Anne Frank

18

Pretoria

'Each time I think that the song is ended ... something higher and better begins for me.'

Hans Christian Andersen

Bryce was back in Isaiah because bits of it had brought him more comfort than anything else, in the fifteen months since France. Verse two of chapter forty-three was already underlined – probably by whomever the Bible had belonged to, before Jules – but he asterisked the margin anyway because he wanted the verse branded into his brain. A truth tattoo telling the story of his grief and healing.

'When you go through deep waters, I will be with you. When you go through rivers of difficulty, you will not drown. When you walk through the fire of oppression, you will not be burned up; the flames will not consume you.'

There was a knock on his office door.

He closed the book and slipped it back into the leather bag Jules had always teased him about. *#ManBag*, he thought. He didn't often read the Bible at the office, but he always carried it with him.

Soon after Jules's death, Bryce had been pragmatic about her things, the way she would've been. *#ItsJustStuff*, he could hear her say. He kept her special jewellery, her most precious books, for when the kids were older. He kept the love letters and photo albums. The girls each chose one of her scarves, which they draped near their pillows and clutched and stroked during tearful bedtime prayer and snuggle sessions. David took a pair of her gloves: 'So I can still hold Mommy's hand.' He knew some might think these gestures macabre, but he'd prayed for wisdom. Scarves and gloves had come to mind. And, all things considered, the kids were managing.

Beth had helped Bryce with the rest of Jules's things, giving them away to friends and charities with a flawless efficiency he couldn't have mustered. But the Bible was the one piece of his wife he allowed himself to hold. She'd loved it so quickly and so deeply, those last few days of her life. And, he knew, it was the timelessness of Scripture that helped him keep on keeping on instead of floundering between grief (on days he couldn't carry on without her) and guilt (on days he could). It reminded him she was alive in his future.

And more and more, he was finding his way out of despair, through the Word. He discovered he could plot a course – almost algebraically – through his heartache. He could find the way because Jesus called Himself *the way*. And Bryce knew Jesus. So Bryce knew the way. He could navigate. He could hope.

Again he'd prayed for wisdom, lying alone on the vast island of their king-size bed in those first pain-wracked months, and God had answered.

Pretoria.

It made sense. Jules's mom and dad had been divorced for ten years, each estranged from the wider family. They barely tolerated Bryce. Their every aloof comment had stung Jules and left Bryce seething. They were token – mostly absent – grandparents. Bryce needed his folks, and so did the kids. With the bulk of his clients in Gauteng anyway, it was an easy and obvious decision to sell the house in Glen Ashley and relocate.

Another thing he didn't often do at the office was see clients so late in the day. It was just about time to collect the kids from his parents' place. But Katlego, his receptionist, had scheduled an appointment because, 'Sorry

Bryce, the lady couldn't come earlier.'

'Come in.' He stood up, glancing down at a portfolio report that would need his attention the next day.

'Mr McIntosh?' He looked up. A young woman – blonde, far too thin, and holding the door ajar – had not quite stepped into his office. 'Hello.'

'Hi,' he said, and again, 'Come in.'

'Thank you. And thank you for seeing me so late in the day.' She spoke too quickly, but very eloquently. 'Your receptionist said you really prefer earlier appointments but I work in Midrand and I couldn't get off any sooner so – '

'No problem at all,' said Bryce. 'Sit down, please.' He didn't know what he'd expected when Katlego had scrawled an appointment brief that said something like, *Non-profit looking for corporate social responsibility funding – more efficient channels.* But this woman wasn't it.

'You must be – ' he looked down again – moved his iPad and the portfolio report – 'Kayla. Kayla Ray.'

Kayla nodded and smiled. She was nervous. She'd heard Bryce McIntosh was the person who would know what to do. And here she was.

She watched him. He skimmed through something on his tablet screen and she wondered if he would know where to begin righting the wrongs, and if the wrongs she wanted to right would mean much at all to a man like him.

'So, you have some funding queries. Sorry – you're with *which* non-profit?'

'Oh no, I don't work for a non-profit. I do staff training and some copywriting for Tech-Tree. It's an IT company. And it has nothing to do with trees. Which is part of the problem.'

Bryce laughed. She was delightful. *Gosh, she's young,* he thought. *Gen-Z?* Yet something about her led him to contemplate briefly how some people didn't fit neatly between the cultural or chronological parameters assigned to them. They weren't Boomers or Generation Xers or Millennials. They were just *perennials*: more flexible, and comfortable to connect an assortment of generational dots. He suspected this woman wouldn't want to be cast in a mould. There was something classic about her fluid movements, her authenticity and poise.

'Ok, you're going to have to backup a bit. I'm not sure I'm following. Katlego said you were from a non-profit – in need of corporate funding.'

'Sorry – I probably wasn't crystal clear on the phone. Thing is – I'm not particularly happy in my current position – '

'You hate your job,' Bryce corrected her with a slow nod.

Kayla's eyes widened – surprised – and she laughed. 'Yes, that would probably be more accurate. The people are mostly ok, but it's just not me. I am one hundred percent un-passionate about software and licence agreements and, well, money-making in general. Sorry. No offence. I mean, money is your thing. Which is why I need your help. I heard about you – through friends of friends – Jean and Laurie? – they're at Hope Church – which is where you go – I think?'

'Ok,' Bryce was still nodding, and smiling now, because this was certainly the most colourful client conversation he'd had all day. Maybe all year. And yes, Hope Church was where his parents had been for years and while he wasn't quite ready to join a men's prayer meeting or volunteer for barista duty, he and the kids had slotted in quickly. It was safe. It felt home-ish.

'And I know you generally only see huge important corporate clients and all, so again, thank you for making the time. You see, the thing is – ' She stopped.

'What is the thing?' Bryce was leaning forward.

Kayla gave another nervous laugh. 'The thing is, I want to *start* a non-profit. And I'm completely prepared for you to tell me it's crazy and impossible, in which case I will leave, and say thank-you-once-again-for-your-time. But I keep asking myself, "Ten years from now, what will I regret *not* doing, if I don't do it now?" And, well, I have nothing to lose. Like, *nothing*.'

'I'm listening.' And he was.

'So, um,' she sighed. 'I've got a Master's in English and Communication. I lectured a bit at UCT – hence the training and copywriting now. I have a bit of money saved but not much – like, fifty-two thousand? And a retirement annuity and that stuff. And what I really want to do – *all* I really want to do – is wage peace.'

'Wage peace?' said Bryce.

'Yes.' Kayla nodded like this was not a juxtaposition. 'I mean – it's just that – I've been thinking about suffering. And changing the world. And God could end suffering right now if He chose to, not so? Except, then He would have to end *us*. Because we're part of the problem. We inflict suffering on ourselves, on others, on the environment. So instead of God pouring petrol on the world and throwing a match over his shoulder and forgetting the chaos we've caused – instead of *removing* us – He chose to *redeem* us. And I want to be part of that.'

Bryce was quiet. His eyes didn't leave her face. She shifted self-consciously.

'And I get it, I'm only twenty-eight – well, almost twenty-eight – and maybe that's not old enough to have serious opinions about humanity, but I've noticed that people change out of desperation or inspiration. Because they have to, or because they want to. And I want to inspire people to change – I want them to *want* to change – because changed hearts change behaviour. And changed behaviour changes society. And I've tried some social awareness stuff like spoken word poetry, but it felt so lame, in like an angsty, shouty sort of way? And I would just lie in bed cringing afterwards and hoping I wouldn't get tagged in any Facebook posts.'

Bryce laughed. 'I've never been one for angsty, shouty poetry myself.'

'So, like – I know it's become a bit of a clichéd example – but you know the whole Rudy Giuliani thing? He was the – '

'Mayor of New York City,' finished Bryce, swallowing hard because a lump may or may not have begun to form in his throat.

'Exactly!' said Kayla. 'You know the rest. And I'm thinking about dustbins and eco-education and street galleries of wall art on inner city buildings – '

Bryce's phone rang.

'I'm so sorry,' he glanced at Kayla. 'Ma! Hi... Oh gosh... Can you stop it?... So d'you reckon – ja... Ok... Of course... I'll be there in ten minutes.'

Kayla wore a look of candid concern and Bryce took note that though she was waif-like and young, in under three decades her soul had been somewhere very far away, and back again. Here was a woman of substance and obvious conviction. She carried a story in her slender body, and he wanted to hear it.

'Is everything ok?' she asked, standing up and slinging her handbag over a shoulder because clearly their meeting had just been urgently terminated.

'I'm very sorry, Kayla. Uh. Stitches, probably. My son David.' Bryce was calm. Focused. Half-smiling, even. 'Nothing too drastic – just something about his forehead colliding with a doorframe at full five-year-old tilt.'

'Oh wow.'

Bryce was gathering his things too. 'I'll head out with you,' he said. 'Just – two things. Firstly, go and read first Timothy four verse twelve. Because you need to own this idea. Secondly, can we reschedule this meeting? Do you get a lunch break? Tomorrow? There's something specific we need to discuss.'

'Ok. First Timothy four twelve. And ok. Yes. Lunch. What do we need to discuss?' she asked, turning to Bryce as he ushered her from the office.

He smiled.

'Litter.'

October
2 0 1 9

*'You've got to remember: we don't know when and how
we are leaving the greatest marks on the world.
It all matters. Believe it: Every tremor of kindness
might erupt in a miracle on the other side of the world.'*

Ann Voskamp

19

Atlanta

'May your choices reflect your hopes, not your fears.'

Nelson Mandela

Even when Thandeka didn't need groceries, she spent pretty much every Friday morning in Publix. Sometimes – like today – she would take a trolley (which she'd learned to call a *shopping cart*) and wheel it slowly up... slowly down... every aisle... for an unnecessarily long time, eventually arriving at a checkout with only two or three items. She did this because the free WiFi in Publix was *reliably* reliable, and she used it to call or text Drew.

Jerusalem had happened more than two years ago, and Drew had pursued her passionately, cheerfully, flirtatiously, seriously, relentlessly, ever since. Their relationship had begun to rise on a tide of emails, texts, video chats, late-night calls and two surprise visits from Drew to Atlanta.

Thandeka had done everything in her power to swim against the current of his love – until about six months ago, when she finally stopped fighting the feeling. Instead, she let herself go with the powerful flow, at last admitting to herself – and then to Drew – that he was all she wanted.

Now as she wandered down an aisle of chips – crackers – popcorn – her mind livestreamed that wave of events:

Gogo gets sick at the beginning of April. Really sick. Sick enough for Thandeka's cousin, Nofoto, to call: 'I think you must come.' And so she takes leave from the day care centre where she works, Monday to Thursday, and meets with her study supervisor to rearrange some assignment dates for her course in early childhood development. She's already fast-tracked to finish by the end of the summer, so it's, 'Sure, no problem.' She boards a plane and the familiar smells and sounds and vibrations of a pressurised cabin make her feel already-halfway-home.

Drew has moved to Pretoria. He's working for an architecture firm in Brooklyn. Thandeka fully expects him to take the morning off to meet her at O.R. Tambo, and he does. She falls into his arms and ugly-cries. What she hasn't expected is for him to have a bag with him.

'What's that now?' she asks, pointing to the carryon at his feet when eventually she lets go of him and wipes his wet neck with the back of her hand. 'Sorry.'

'I'm coming with you.' And for the first time in their shared history, she offers no protestations. He's booked himself onto her connecting flight to Durban. He messages Nofoto to say she needn't fetch Thandeka at the airport because he's hired a car, and he drives Thandeka – jet-lagged, bewildered, strangely relieved – to Nkwazela, the Drakensberg stretching across the horizon before them like the hug of home.

Thandeka enters the old house – even older, and much smaller, than she remembers it. The moment she sees gogo – shrunken – shallow breaths barely lifting her chest – she knows her grandmother is dying.

'Thandeka.' Gogo's voice is still formidable but there's a smile tucked into it. 'You came. So far. You shouldn't have come. You're a good girl, Thandeka.'

Thandeka bursts into fresh tears, which dissolve the last of the inevitable culture shock that always rocks her upon return. She kneels next to the bed and rests her head on the cool sheets, because these are words she's waited all her life to hear.

'Gogo,' she wails, 'I'm sorry I've been so far. I'm so sorry. I should've – '

'Stop your tears now. Stop crying,' fusses gogo with a soft chuckle that morphs into a cough. Her rheumy eyes find Thandeka. 'I want to see your white boy.'

For a moment Thandeka doesn't know what to say. She half-laughs, half-cries, which Drew calls 'craughing.' Her face is hot. 'Gogo! I – he's – '

'Nofoto told me. He's here.'

'Hello, gogo.' Drew is suddenly kneeling next to Thandeka. She knows he's been standing in the doorway of the dim room, unsure of his place in the moment. He gently takes one of gogo's hands – thin, dry, smooth as paper – in his. 'I'm so honoured to meet you,' he says with a tenderness that brings on Thandeka's tears again and she thinks, Who are you? *as she looks at the magnificent, kind, incredibly attractive man at her side who for reasons she can't fathom, loves her unimaginably.*

Drew exchanges charming pleasantries with gogo, in Zulu, as if he's grown up in the village and Thandeka thinks, Of course, you've learned Zulu. You would. *Then Drew says, 'Would you mind if I pray for you?' Thandeka has never felt the freedom to pray with her grandmother – to minister to her – and she's so glad Drew has come and she sees something soften in gogo's expression and she realises the iron will has been replaced by fondness – peace – readiness.*

It's while Drew is praying for the old woman who has loved and raised her that the wave finally crashes on the beachhead of Thandeka's resistance and all the reasons she's been unwilling to surrender completely to the idea of a future with him are washed forever out to sea.

Because up to this point, she's been thrashing out opposing arguments between herself and herself, and also, between herself and God.

He's white. (Seriously? Like that matters.)

He's three years younger than me. (And your point is…?)

He has a past. (Correction. He *had* a past – which I dealt with on the cross. In much the same way I dealt with *your* past, Thandeka. And remember – *gogo* gave her life so your past needn't determine your future.)

Gogo dies that night.

Drew helps with food and phone calls and funeral arrangements. He fries chicken and chops carrots and lays starched tablecloths on trestle tables and kicks soccer balls in the dust with kids who keep appearing and he pretends not to notice all the staring and giggling that Thandeka and her cousins are doing, like, all the time.

'Eish, Drew,' Thandeka says worriedly. 'You know this is a black funeral, right? These things can — '

'I've taken enough leave,' he laughs. 'It's chilled. I want to be here.' And he lets her cry a little more. She knows he desperately wants to hold her. But they're in Nkwazela, not Joburg or Jerusalem, and it's just not done.

When it's all over and the community finally begins to disperse and Thandeka has taken selfies with all her cousins and hugged them hard, Drew drives her back to Durban. Her grief is raw but she's wide awake to him, to his love. Drew can't stop smiling. Then he feels bad because, gogo. But then he's smiling and smiling and talking and smiling and telling her more about his new life in Pretoria and all the ways it intersects with his old life in Joburg and she wants him to go on talking and talking and smiling and she's smiling too.

He gets a text — glances down at his phone even though they're on the highway now. 'No way!' He tells her about reconnecting with a friend at church — a girl he grew up with. She was shot in an armed robbery — nearly five years ago — and she can't have kids and something about the story feels familiar to Thandeka, but then again, she's read too much tragic news. Same crimes. Different names and places. Drew says he's so stoked because this friend met someone — an older guy with kids — and the whole thing just drips with redemption. 'So anyway, that was her, and they just got engaged!'

Drew tells her how Kayla — that's the girl — she's been pretty stressed about the age gap — fourteen years — 'So three years is nothing, babe,' he jokes — and properly *stressed about three instant kids even though she totally gets how they're an extravagant gift. 'The other day she was like, "Drew, I'm too young to be mothering three humans!" And I was like, "Remember Romeo and Juliet?" (Because both our schools did it when we were in Grade 10.) Paris tells Juliet's dad to chill out because even though Juliet's only thirteen, "Younger than she are happy mothers made." And I just said to her, "Friend, so much has been stolen from you; don't let this chance slip away too."'*

It's while they're waiting at King Shaka International Airport — to board a flight back to Joburg where Thandeka will have four hours to kill before her Delta flight back to

Atlanta – that Drew begs her to stay:

'Please.'

It isn't even a question – more a quiet, vulnerable confession. And she doesn't tease and object and laugh it off. Just takes his hands. Closes her eyes. Rests her head against his chest. And after a while she says, 'Not yet. I need to finish this thing, you know? For me, for gogo. She worked so hard so me and my cousins – we could have a future – and – ' She can't go on.

'I know,' whispers Drew. 'Ok.'

Absentmindedly, Thandeka put a box of microwave popcorn into her Publix cart and it pulled her back into the present and she smiled because she *had*. She had *finished this thing*. She'd qualified with a preschool teaching diploma and she was working out her notice period at the day care centre. She hadn't told Drew yet, that she'd resigned. She was waiting for the right moment to break the happy news that there was no longer anything, officially, keeping her stateside.

After *gogo*'s death, she'd taken her grief and her love back to Atlanta with her and although she was part of a great church, and although she had sweet colleagues and a fistful of beautiful friends, she wanted to take her grief and her love back home, where it would be completely seen, and completely safe. She wanted to take it back home because she'd realised home wasn't a place but a person.

She knew it was already late at night, for Drew. She knew he wouldn't mind. She texted –

Music loud in here today – I'll phone tomorrow?

Sure, he replied. **What you buying?**

Popcorn and a new toothbrush. You know they have a whole aisle JUST for peanut butter – insane.

It salved them both to text each other random news from their days.

Drew replied with ROFL emojis, and –

What flavour popcorn? I made biryani for supper – just the DIY box from Pick 'n Pay. But still delish. And then, **Where's my quote, baby?**

Because interspersed with these mundanities, their conversation history held links to podcast episodes, screenshots from their Kindle apps, copy-paste excerpts of articles and blogposts they'd each been reading, and Deep Quotes. They'd facetiously been playing the Deep Quote Game every day for the past few months. Drew had already texted –

Quote of the day, here goes. From Robert Frost – stoic and fatalistic – but also comforting? 'In three words, I can sum up everything I've learned about life. It goes on.'

Thandeka stood still in the dental care aisle, reading Drew's texts and grinning something silly.

Ok ok! She texted. **Patience… Here it is – from Leonard Bernstein – though it's not that deep actually. You win today. 'To achieve great things, two things are needed; a plan, and not quite enough time.' Oh – butter popcorn.**

Nice! The quote and the flavour. Replied Drew. Her app told her he was *Typing…* She typed too –

Ok I better pay, meeting Vanessa at Waffle House now-now. Love you miss you madly chat tomorrow xxx

She was still smiling. She waited.

Wait! He texted. She laughed out loud.

'Can I help you, ma'am?' asked a polite Publix employee with a large, luminous badge that said KEVIN – HERE TO HELP. He looked about twelve but was probably twenty and she knew what he meant was, 'Why are you grinning, and standing still in this aisle? Why have you been here for forty minutes, and you're only buying two items?'

'All good. Thanks so much,' she turned her radiant smile and exotic accent on Kevin-Here-to-Help and like most mortals, it left him dazed and powerless and happy for her to block the aisle for as long as she needed to.

Drew was still *Typing...* Then:

Speaking of greatness and plans and not enough time, you still haven't let me know about being my plus 1 at Kayla's wedding – which will be GREAT, just so you know, but we need a PLAN and there's not a lot of TIME... Please please please please please you know you want to. Can I buy your ticket? Please please please please.

She was still smiling before a wall of toothpaste and floss options while Kevin-Here-to-Help hovered nearby – fake-repacking a shelf that didn't need repacking – basking in her beauty and desperately hoping she might need something.

Don't buy me a ticket, she texted.

She scrolled through her emails for the airline's confirmation.

Screen shot. Share. Send. Then –

So do I need a new dress? Is this wedding black tie, smart casual, what?

20

Pretoria

'...the present is the point at which time touches eternity.'

C.S. Lewis

It rains the night before the wedding – the first real rains of spring – and the expansive lawns of Hope Church are a glorious lilac mess of jacaranda blooms. The photos will be magnificent. The deep blue bright sky is washed of highveld dust. There will be no rain today and the world feels perfect.

God breathes over, between, in and through the people and the preparations, which start just after dawn because the bride will walk down the petaled aisle at ten o'clock. Chairs are set out in rows on the damp grass beneath the trees. There's a make-it-official makeshift stage and flowered canopy. Beneath more spreading trees are low, wooden-pallet tables and cushions and quilts. There will be platters piled high with fruit and fresh things, cupcakes and cream.

The caterer's name is Goodwin Chiyangwa, and he's brought along two of his best baristas, Kutenda and Famous. His sister, Aneni, is helping too. Goodwin doesn't usually do weddings – he's a casual, coffee truck kind of guy – but a client of the groom's mother's hairdresser has tasted his coffees and his canapés, at the Neighbourgoods Market. She raves so much, the groom himself, Bryce McIntosh, tracks him down and begs him.

'Nothing fancy. It's a morning wedding. Light snacks. Sublime coffee. You in?' Goodwin is always looking to learn and serve and willingly comes through from Joburg to make it happen.

'You're going to tell me we're here because we're "blessed to be a blessing", aren't you?' says Aneni, teasing him because he's all about the Christian clichés, but there's no hidden hook in her words. She's been secretly experimenting with the idea that he may be right. Goodwin laughs and watches her drizzling balsamic reduction over crudités. She's stunning. He wishes their mom could see her now, so he pulls out his phone – 'Smile!' – and sends a bajillion beautiful pixels north through the airwaves.

The worship team is tuning and practising, unplugged. There's laughter and banter and a bit of posing by singers and guitarists. Goodwin is watching the drummer – a boy. Well, almost a man. Fifteen, sixteen? He's exceptional. After a run-through of the songs ('Awesome, guys, that's a wrap,' says the worship leader in a cool, gravelly voice) the drummer wanders past the table Goodwin has set up near his van to put finishing touches on the platters. The kid's tapping his sticks on his thighs, rhythm evidently still thrumming through his soul.

'Excuse me,' says Goodwin to the boy, and the sticks take a beat. 'Would you mind tasting this, please?' He offers an éclair. 'I'm not sure they're any good. What's your name?'

'I'm JD,' replies the boy, mouth already full. 'These are amazing!'

'Whew!' smiles Goodwin. 'Otherwise, big problems today. I'm Goodwin. You're an excellent drummer, JD.'

JD grins and says he's not supposed to be drumming today. He's a last-minute addition. The *real* drummer is about to become a dad. 'They're friends of mine – Reuben and Nadia – and she went into labour at two this morning, or something like that. So Reuben messaged me, like, two hours ago, and asked me to fill in. I actually drummed at *their* wedding too, which is kinda cool.'

'I think you're definitely supposed to be drumming today,' declares Goodwin.

'Me too, I guess,' nods JD with a smile.

'I'm no expert. Just the coffee guy. Yet still I can tell you're not a one-talent drummer or a two-talent drummer. You're a five-talent drummer. But you already know that, don't you?' Goodwin looks intently at JD who blushes and grins. 'I hope I get to download you on iTunes one day, so I can listen to how you turn five into ten.'

JD swallows his éclair, and some emotion. He thanks Goodwin and thinks about the church in London he and his mom will be joining a month from now. Every time he goes onto the website and clicks on the 'worship' tab his stomach flips with wondrous, nervous hope. He thinks of what Reuben has told him: 'Kindness and courage, dude. Pack those and you'll be fine. And you can't miss your calling, my man. Impossible! Just stay close enough to the Father to hear His voice, calling you.'

Help me be kind. Help me be brave. Help me stay close, he prays. And bright, familiar words – Narnia words that never dive and swim – sit bold and motionless and non-dyslexic before his mind's eye. It's Jewel, the unicorn from *The Last Battle*, but really, it's God answering and singing out a glad invitation to him: *'Come further up, come further in!'*

JD's mom, Lizette, is wiping dust off the chairs and laughing at something Allie is saying. Allie is the bride's mom and the bride's name is Kayla and Kayla is friends with Lizette because they teach the four-year-olds at King's Kids together and JD knows this wedding is going to feel like Facebook in real life: a crisscross of connections both deep and tenuous. Everyone feels like a friend, or at least a friend suggestion.

For the longest time nothing has worked out for Lizette and JD to move to London even though they believe it's in their future. But Lizette keeps casting vision, hope and patience. She reminds JD, 'God's never late.' JD hates waiting but he knows she's right and then Lizette gets a bolt-from-the-blue call from an employment agency. There's a church in King's Cross advertising a position – admin and accounts – and she's the perfect fit. And JD can see they probably weren't ready before now and yes, God's never late.

'Hello, boy,' says Lizette, throwing down her cloth and hugging him. 'You sounded incredible. Ooh hang on.' Her phone buzzes in her bag, slung over a chair. 'It's Reuben!' JD's phone buzzes too. 'It's a girl!' shrieks Lizette and JD isn't even that embarrassed because it's pretty rad that a brand new human's little lungs have just sucked air for the first time, and according to the proud new dad, the brand new human has already found her voice.

'Hey, Train Man!' JD turns to see Drew making his way towards them over the lawn, smiling a mile wide. 'D'you get Reuben's text? Awesome, hey?' JD still feels a bit starstruck and a bit what-are-the-chances when he's around Drew.

It's almost a year since the night JD was baptised. The night he was sitting near the front of the church, near the posse of hot girls. The night a guy sauntered up to the microphone and JD thought, 'There's something about him…' And the guy told a story of Jesus tenderly wrenching him right out of his rebellion and how he was baptised in Lake Malawi and how God had helped him to forgive his dad and he said a bunch of other stuff and then he said, 'I want you to know everything's going to be ok,' and JD remembered being rescued on a train by those same words, and by words on a left-behind page that stilled his heaving soul.

That night Drew said into the mic, 'If you feel God has been speaking to you about baptism – ' and JD didn't wait for the rest of the appeal. He kicked off his slops and headed to the baptism pool and Drew was there, grinning in boardshorts, ready to dunk the keen, in the name of the Father, Son and Holy Spirit. He stared at JD. 'No way. No freakin' way!' And JD flung his arms around Drew and sobbed with pent up gratitude.

'Walk with me, JD,' Drew says today. 'I've got to get the rings to Bryce. He's in the guesthouse. They were Kayla's grandparents. They melted them down and had them re-set. Super special.' Drew is smiling *a lot*.

'Why are you so – oh! Ha!' laughs JD. 'Your girlfriend's arriving!'

'Any minute! She was supposed to arrive last night and I was supposed to fetch her – obviously! – but her flight was delayed and she only landed at six this morning, and I'd promised to pick up the rings this morning because the jeweller left things to the *very* last minute, apparently, so it's been panic stations all round, gosh. But my mom fetched her from the airport – and met her for the first time! So like, no pressure and all. And they've been getting wedding-ready at my mom's place.' Drew adds seriously, a hand on JD's shoulder: 'So listen, just try and hold it together when you see her. She's overwhelmingly beautiful.' JD laughs and Drew asks (properly seriously this time) as they walk across the lawn towards the church guesthouse normally used by visiting preachers and home-on-leave missionaries: 'So how was the spot-your-talent thing?'

JD lets out a long sigh. 'Yoh. Intense.' He's just come through three nights in a row of a spiritual gifts workshop. He wasn't interested in going but Reuben and Nadia were very interested on his behalf and signed him up. 'You have to go. If you don't, it will upset me and that's not good for the baby,' Nadia said, stroking her belly dramatically, and laughing. 'Such manipulation,' JD said, shaking his head. He showed up. So did God.

'So?' asks Drew, his excitement levels showing no signs of waning. 'I want the deets!'

JD says, 'Um, turns out I've got a bit of a prophecy thing going on.' He feels suddenly awkward and shoves his drumsticks into his jeans pockets and kicks at jacaranda flowers in the grass as they walk.

'That's flippin' incredible, Train Man!'

177

JD laughs. 'I dunno. I mean, it's not like I'm Nostradamus or anything.'

'How are you feeling about London?' Drew has been slowing down and now they stop. 'New school, new church, new everything?'

'Excited. Terrified.'

'All normal,' Drew nods.

'And expectant. I mean, I'm still going to be dyslexic on the other side of the world. But I just *know* it's right, you know? Which makes all the goodbye trauma a bit easier at least. And it's weird – I don't know if this makes any sense – but I have this feeling – '

Drew grins. 'Come on! Prophesy!'

'Ha! Ok. Well. I just have this feeling the world is on the edge of something.'

'You haven't gone all flat-earth-society on me, have you, dude?'

JD cracks up. 'No! And listen, I'm not about to tweet this, and it actually sounds totally cray when I say it out loud. It's just that, well, the world has become really small, right? With the internet and whatever. And we're all super connected. And so, if something big were to happen to the world – like say, a global pandemic that makes loads of people sick and shuts down economies and stuff – I mean, I'm sure that can't happen – but if it did, it would affect all of us. And I feel like the church is going to rise up and meet this thing, and again, I have no idea what it is, but I want to be ready, and I think us going to London is part of that.'

Drew listens. He's amazed and inspired by this boy who, ironically, he knows, is amazed and inspired by him. Scriptures come to mind. Zechariah saying, *'Do not despise these small beginnings,'* and Paul writing to Timothy, *'Don't let anyone think less of you because you are young.'* He says, 'JD, don't stop praying about this stuff. Pray for wisdom and discernment. And just promise me you'll stay in touch from your side of the equator, when whatever is going to happen to the world, happens?'

'For sure,' smiles JD.

Bryce wanders out of the guesthouse to meet them, in a t-shirt and boxers. 'Dude, you didn't have to get all dressed up for us,' jokes Drew, foraging in his pockets for the tiny organza drawstring pouch containing two perfect, white gold rings.

'Think nothing of it!' grins Bryce. 'You're the best, Drew, seriously. Thanks a million. All good out there in wedding world? Gosh, everyone's slaving away and I'm swanning about in my undies. Can't I do something?'

'You could get dressed,' suggests Drew. 'It's all systems go in twenty minutes.'

'Ah! I knew there was something! Ok guys, thanks again.'

'Check you now-now, dude. You're a lucky man.' Drew hugs Bryce and slaps him on the back to make it more of a manly experience because he's quite overcome with emotion.

JD says, 'Drew? Um, I think – '

Drew turns away from Bryce who heads inside for pants and a shirt, and there she is. And temporarily, Drew can't breathe or speak.

'Hello, I'm JD,' says JD, extending a hand, because he figures someone needs to be the grownup. 'You must be Thandeka. I'm so sorry, Drew isn't usually so rude.'

Drew recovers from the shock of Thandeka's 3D, real-life beauty to which he hasn't been exposed for too many long months, and he's laughing and holding her and she's also laughing and JD can totally see why Drew is so crazy for this woman wearing pink silk and a perfect smile.

'Hello Helen,' says JD. A big believer in giving people space, Drew's mom has casually, respectfully, taken five good long minutes to lock up her car… before joining them outside the guesthouse.

'Howzit ma!' Drew hugs her too, beaming. 'So do you completely love my lady or what? Thank you for rescuing her!'

Helen laughs. 'Yes, my boy, I do completely love her. I also feel completely sorry for her! I wish I could have organised eight hours of sleep for her as easily I organised the hot shower.' She looks sympathetically at Thandeka, who is still leaning against Drew. She's radiating happiness despite the jetlag.

'I better get back,' says JD. 'I think they're starting soon. Catch you later! Very nice to meet you, Thandeka.' He jogs back towards the official ceremony zone beneath the trees, tapping his drumsticks on his thighs again as he runs. Drew, Thandeka and Helen follow slowly. Drew clutches Thandeka's hand, mesmerized and smiling and asking her questions she's too tired to answer and Helen laughs at him again, 'Drew! Let her breathe! You've got time.'

The band is playing. People take their seats and there's the hushed twitter of expectation and Bryce has arrived too: resplendent, handsome, happy (and fully clothed). Thandeka's presence has caused Drew's usually suave, time-sensitive, social and relational filters to malfunction and he whispers to her, 'Listen, I know you've been in the country for like, three minutes, but babe, here's my Deep Quote of the day, by yours truly: "I just can't anymore."'

'That's your Deep Quote?' she whispers back, suppressing a laugh.

'Yes. I can't anymore. I can't do this long-distance thing. I mean, if – '

'You don't have to. I'm here.'

'But your job – '

'Resigned a month ago. One-way ticket,' she smiles. 'Surprise!' Drew exhales and it feels like he's been holding his breath for a century. 'The details are sketchy,' she says. 'Your mom has already insisted I stay with her for a while. But what I'm actually going to do with the rest of my life remains a mystery.'

'You're going to marry me, at long freakin' last!' Drew says in a stage whisper. An elderly man in front of them turns and stares. 'That's what you're going to do with the rest of your life,' he says less loudly. 'And of course, anything else you dream.'

It's just after ten. The band takes it up a notch. This is it.

Bethel released their *Victory* album four months after Bryce and Kayla met, and for Kayla, one song became the soundtrack of their vibing, their Facebook-official, their engagement. She wants today to be worship, from beginning to end. So even though some people will think it's weird, she's chosen to walk down the aisle with everyone looking at Jesus, not looking at her.

The congregation stands, and starts to sing –

I love You, Lord
For Your mercy never fails me
All my days, I've been held in Your hands
From the moment that I wake up
Until I lay my head
Oh, I will sing of the goodness of God
'Cause all my life You have been faithful
And all my life You have been so, so good
With every breath that I am able
Oh, I will sing of the goodness of God…

The worship team is suddenly all smiles, and everyone turns to see Mia (focused), David (distracted) and Leila (ecstatic) ambling down the aisle in slow, practised steps, and still the people sing –

I love Your voice
You have led me through the fire
And in darkest night You are close like no other
I've known You as a Father
I've known You as a Friend

And I have lived in the goodness of God…

The music swells and there's no one who isn't struggling to sing through their tears because, Kayla.

'Cause Your goodness is running after, it's running after me
Your goodness is running after, it's running after me
With my life laid down, I'm surrendered now
I give You everything
'Cause Your goodness is running after, it's running after me

She's glorious in white lace and her dad's cheeks are wet as he walks her into the future but she's just smiling and looking into the faces of friends and family and their voices carry her. Then she's looking at Bryce and catching her breath because she can't believe she'll get to wake up next to him for as long as they're both breathing. She holds a bouquet of lavender to match the jacarandas at her feet. 'For Jules,' she whispers when she reaches the end of the aisle and slips an arm through his.

Someone preaches from Ephesians – something about marriage, and the church being the spotless bride of Christ – but Bryce doesn't hear much, on account of being enraptured by the living, breathing bride by his side.

Aneni hears every word. She's standing a little way away, behind the last row of chairs, with Goodwin, who doesn't recognise the bride because five years, true love and a magnificent wedding dress have transformed the girl who used to sip Sprites and Americanos in Camps Bay. Goodwin is relaxed – worshiping and praying and nodding like he's a son in this family, not a servant arranging the food. Aneni feels awkward and uninvited, but wholly intrigued.

There's a woman seated near the back, on the aisle. She must be in her late fifties. Exquisite and elegant. At some point during the service, she turns slowly in her seat. Looks straight into Aneni's eyes. She gets up discreetly and moves to the back.

Why is she coming to me? thinks Aneni, confused and embarrassed.

'Hello dear,' whispers the woman. 'Could I chat to you?' She takes Aneni's hand and leads her a little further away from the ceremony so as not to disturb. Goodwin doesn't notice. His eyes are closed in prayer.

'I'm sorry ma'am,' stammers Aneni. *Where's Kutenda?* 'Is it something with the food? Let me call my – '

'No dear, the food looks marvellous,' says the woman. 'It's you I want to talk to. I'm Helen. What's your name?'

'Aneni.'

'Forgive me for being so forward – and in the middle of this special day! But I'm seldom wrong about these things and I feel you need to know this very minute that your Heavenly Father sees you, and loves you unimaginably.'

And so it is that Aneni, in a server's apron, crosses the Kingdom threshold clothed in the righteousness of a flawless daughter of the Most High. She and Helen miss the rest of the service. Helen prays with her and cries with her. Then, to ease Aneni's self-consciousness – the inevitable aftermath of a spiritual experience – Helen tells her how she's leaving in a week for Malawi.

'My son, Drew, worked with some missionaries in Monkey Bay a few years ago. They're connected to our church in Joburg, and they've reached out to us for help with their women's ministry. I've done a bit of that, here and there, and I don't have all that much going on in Joburg, at the moment. Well, until my daughter has her baby in March! They're sitting near the front there – Mark and Stella – I'll introduce you just now. So I figured I'd head up there and help out for a few months. Are you alright, dear?'

'Monkey Bay?' Aneni looks like she's been slapped.

'Yes, that's right,' says Helen. 'Let me find you a glass of water.'

'No it's ok,' says Aneni. The flicker of a smile arrives in her eyes.

'Would it be possible, do you think, for someone like me to come with you? I'm just helping my brother today. I don't really have a lot going on in Joburg either. But I've got money saved. I used to work there too, in Monkey Bay, and the women – ' she takes a deep breath. 'The women I worked with, they need to know also that God sees them and loves them.'

The ceremony is over. There's whooping and clapping and you-may-kiss-the-bride and then someone is reminding the guests that gifts have been strictly prohibited in favour of donations to Adopt a Block and Fill a Bin which are part of Kayla's non-profit. She rolled out the initiative eight months ago and it's transforming the capital city from the inside out. Kayla has been approached by three other metros because the idea of a municipal makeover is making waves.

Bryce and Kayla can't get enough of looking at each other with undiluted joy, relief, desire. Then they're flooded with hugs, kisses, high-fives and fist bumps. It's Drew and Thandeka's turn to congratulate them.

'Thandeka!' says Kayla. 'It's *so* amazing to finally meet you although I feel like I already know you because Drew talks about you literally *all* the time!' Bryce doesn't recognize Thandeka, but she's been piecing it all together, and she remembers. The day in Amboise. The flight from Paris. In time, perhaps, they'll talk about it. Today she hugs them both and says, 'I'm so happy to be here. Congratulations!'

Someone hands Kayla a bottle of water, which she realises she desperately needs. There's music and mingling and family photos and it's starting to feel like a party.

'Babe, remind me of the caterer's name?' Kayla says to Bryce. She's watching him weave through the crowd with unhurried, smiling decorum. He looks familiar. They've been to the Neighbourgoods Market a few times. She's probably seen him there.

'Goodwin Chiyangwa.'

'Goodwin?' Obviously from Zim. Her brain skips a beat. She feels herself pale, but she doesn't know why.

'You ok my love?' asks Bryce, concerned. 'Should we sit down for a while?'

'Don't worry. I think it's just the heat. And the intense pressure of being bridal,' she says with a dazzling smile, her mind protectively misplacing the memory once again.

Kayla's physical recovery from the shooting took more than a year. Her emotional and spiritual healing have taken much longer. She still can't remember everything about that November day, but time and therapy have dissolved the incapacitating shock. She can breathe deeply again, observing fragments of memory with composure and acceptance. Slowly, the searing, everyday-pain of facing a childless future has subsided into a sometimes-pain. She's chosen – over and over – to walk the steep paths of forgiveness. She's clung to her faith – and slipped – and clung again – and already Bryce and the kids have restored so much of her stolen hope. Still, sometimes a 'Why?' forces its way into her consciousness, despite her brave determination to live a 'What now?' kind of life, and there are days – even this day – when she knows her healing isn't done.

Goodwin is back behind the coffee machine, grinding beans into the portafilter and instructing Famous over his shoulder about refilling platters, which Famous hands to Aneni, who is nodding and smiling, floating on forgiveness, utterly loved.

Goodwin looks up and laughs out loud.

'Well then. Would you like a flat white, or an Americano with pouring cream?'

Thandeka is standing in front of him. She does a doubletake. 'I beg your – ' She's even lovelier than he remembers – calmer, kinder. Recognition rises in her eyes. 'Oh my gosh! I do not believe this! Drew!' She turns to the man trailing just behind her. 'This is the guy – oh my gosh, oh my gosh!'

Drew is undisturbed but intrigued. 'Which guy?' he asks, grinning at Goodwin and shrugging his shoulders. But then he does a doubletake too. 'Oh my – *this guy!* Goodwin?'

Now Goodwin is the one confounded. '*Drew?*' Then he's beaming. 'You're cleaner than I remember!'

'Wait wait wait!' Thandeka is freaking out, in a good way. '*You know* the barista who gave me the Bible that got me saved? And listen,' she turns to Goodwin again, 'I have no idea what happened to that Bible! I lost it a couple of years ago, on a flight or I don't know where. But I am *definitely* going for the pouring cream. And make my coffee strong. And you two have some explaining to do.'

There are tender speeches and toasts and then Kayla throws her lavender bouquet into a crowd of single women. She misjudges and it hurtles right over the gang of hopefuls and lands in the grass at the feet of an attractive thirty-something-year-old woman who studiously avoids the bouquet-throwing at weddings because she thinks it's a stupid superstition but actually because it makes her feel conspicuously desperate and it's taken her fifteen years but she's made peace with being a single mom forever – or not?

'Go mom!' laughs JD, applauding wildly. Lizette picks up the bouquet, smiles, blows a gracious kiss in Kayla's direction, and realises she's surprisingly, blushingly, pleased.

Kayla raises two triumphant fists and shouts happily, 'Woo hoo, Lizzie!' Even though she's the bride and this is the one day in her life when it's legit for her to claim centre-of-attention status, she believes in her bones she's on the periphery of a deeper, wider story that extends far beyond the boundaries of her small self, and into eternity. She's gripped with gratitude for each inimitable person scattered across the lawns, each lost-and-found, staying-and-leaving, matchless story being lived out for the glory of God.

'Look mamma!' It's Leila, laughing so hard she can barely speak. She's lying in the grass, pretending to be a log, and David is rolling her up to Kayla's feet. He's covered in grass too, and squashed jacarandas, and untroubled, in-the-moment mirth.

David and Leila are like little microwaves. Theirs is a quick hot love. A month after Bryce proposed, they started calling her mamma and mommy and mom. Mia is a crockpot: the kind where you wonder if you've switched it on and chosen the right setting, but slowly, slowly, it warms, and cooks something tender. Still, Mia doesn't call Kayla anything.

Kayla bends and scoops Leila into her arms for a grassy hug. 'Where's Mia?' she asks.

'Coming,' says Leila happily. 'She went to get her Dora-Splorer.' Kayla looks up to see Mia meandering towards them through clusters of adults. She stops to hug Beth and Greg, who have flown up from Durban for the wedding. Kayla knows every single one of Beth's songs by heart and it still feels surreal to have Beth's actual cell number in her phone and to have shifted from fan-girl to friend. Mia is calm and confident, the way she always is when she's clasping the straps of her Dora the Explorer backpack.

When Kayla arrived in their lives, Mia appropriated Bryce's Bible – the one that had belonged to Jules. Bryce gladly relinquished it. As he and the kids each grappled, in their individual ways, with the letting-go and the looking-forward, he was relieved Mia had found a conduit of connectedness to Jules which seemed to help her face the prospect of a changing family dynamic. She carries the Bible everywhere, in the Dora backpack, which no one is allowed to touch.

'Hi sweetie,' says Kayla as Mia approaches.

'Hi.'

'Glad you got your bag,' smiles Kayla, and Mia smiles back. She's thankful Kayla never asks to see what's inside though she's pretty sure her dad has told Kayla that it's her mom's old Bible because it seems her dad tells Kayla *everything* which feels weird but it's probably how things have to be if you're going to be like, actual married grownups.

Mia has just turned nine and she's overly responsible and a little too serious. She reminds Kayla of herself, and so she looks for moments to stand on the common ground of their shared temperament. She pulls Mia gently aside – behind a tree – and talks to her alone and like an adult. 'You'll phone us if Leila can't sleep this week? I'm sure she'll be fine if gran lets her sleep on the mattress next to their bed, but just phone us, ok? If you're worried.'

Mia nods sagaciously, happy to be in charge of something. Then she blurts: 'It's still hard to call you mom.'

It's Kayla's turn to nod knowingly. 'Of course it is. Hmm.' *Give me something, Jesus,* she prays, and a memory softly surfaces. 'How about you call me something else entirely. Not my name – because it's weird for you to say it, hey?'

Mia nods again.

'How about you call me Kit Kat? My grampa used to call me that. When I was little he would – '

Mia's eyes widen. *Oh dear,* thinks Kayla. *Maybe not.*

Slowly, Mia shrugs off the backpack. She leans it against the tree. Unzips it. Deliberately, reverently, she slides out the Bible Kayla knows she's got stashed in there. It has a brown, faux leather cover. Kayla's brain short circuits again and she stops breathing. Mia's hands are shaking but she lifts the Bible to Kayla and her voice is shaking too: 'I think my mom would want you to have this. And so would I. And also maybe God.'

Kayla takes it from Mia and the smooth leather in her palms elicits an avalanche of jumbled recollections. She opens it. The dogeared corner of a card escapes from the inside cover. For years it's been untouched, tucked deep inside the tight-fitting book jacket. But recently, slender, curious, nine-year-old fingers have burrowed inside the cover for comfort and tugged at discovery. Kayla slides the card out. Memory courses through her like lightning. Her face feels strange. Mia shouts – 'Dad!' – and Bryce is at her side, steadying her, and she's reading –

2006-11-26

My Kit Kat

Happy birthday.

This comes with so much love to you, as you keep on keeping on, along God's way. What lies ahead for you is anyone's guess, but your Heavenly Father has plotted your course, and He promises this in Psalm 48:14: 'He is our God forever and ever, and He will guide us until we die.'

Life has its ups and downs, and you'll likely experience suffering, shame and rejection. You'll likely be tempted towards rebellion, anger or fear. It's then, in your quest to be free of those things, that you'll need to dig deep for God's truth, so you can discover possibility, purpose, grace, healing, transformation, peace, hope and love – and ultimately, God's glory, and the advancement of His Kingdom, because that's the point of it all.

Keep doing the next right thing – even if that just means taking the next deep breath. Travel light. Don't be afraid to walk off the map. The view is always better from the road less travelled – and life is either a daring adventure, or nothing at all. May His joy be your strength, every step.

Love always,

Grampa

The world goes quiet like it did that day long ago. She doesn't hear Bryce calling for cushions, doesn't feel him helping her down. But she sees it all again. At least, she sees the same splinters of experience her brain has allowed her to retrieve for processing. And this time, she sees something else.

'Babe what's going on? What's going on?' Bryce sounds desperate and suddenly she can hear him. She looks up into his face, fraught with love.

'Sixty-five. Twenty-four. Isaiah.' she says breathlessly and she's already turning pages, clarity rushing back. The words are there where she left them and the page is splashed and stained dark brown with blood and hope and she thinks about the Messiah foretold on this same page and about *His* blood shed for her and how His goodness has been running *after* her and also His goodness has been running *ahead* of her because He has fulfilled His promise –

'I will answer them before they even call to Me. While they are still talking about their needs, I will go ahead and answer their prayers!'

The cappuccinos keep coming and the guests are blithely engrossed in conversations both superficial and profound. They're unaware of the unlikely unearthing of Kayla's past – the shocking grace of full-circle redemption she hardly expects on her wedding day. Bryce holds her and they're speaking in half-sentences, trying to fathom the leather-covered impossibility of what lies in Kayla's lap.

'I just don't know – '

'So this was – '

'Exactly! Mine! So how did – '

Mia quietly strokes Kayla's arm and though she doesn't quite understand what's happening she says without thinking, 'It's ok, mommy.' Bryce shoots Kayla an elated look. Mia adds, 'We don't have to figure it all out today because you're staying forever. We've got the next chapter. I'll help you.'

'Oh sweetie,' breathes Kayla. She lifts the Bible to her cheeks for a moment, then gives it back to Mia. 'Will you and Dora keep this safe for another week, while we're away? Then when we're home, you and I are going to do some real exploring. What do you say?'

The afternoon turns mellow and still no one wants to leave. Bryce and Kayla re-join the mingling and only Mia, following, notices that Kayla is leaning a little more heavily, but entirely happily, on Bryce's shoulder.

Eventually Bryce turns to Kayla. 'Listen, Mrs McIntosh, I would very much like to leave now and get to know you much, *much*, better.'

Blissfully exhausted, Kayla laughs with all the freedom and joy of a bride who knows she's beautiful, and knows she's loved. She looks up at her husband of half a day, laces her fingers behind his neck and says, 'That sounds amazing.'

'So you're ready to get out of here? Is this day over, d'you think?'

She remembers again the blood on the page, and the blood on the cross, and her words echo something of the Saviour's last breath: 'Yes, I believe it's finished. Also, it's only just begun.'

This is the first novel by bestselling nonfiction author
and well-loved speaker, **Dalene Reyburn**.
She and her family make their home under African skies.

For more, visit www.dalenereyburn.com or follow her @deereyburn.

www.ingramcontent.com/pod-product-compliance
Lightning Source LLC
Chambersburg PA
CBHW061231170626
46809CB00007B/2611